MERRY LITTLE MISHAP

✦ A SPICY HOLIDAY ✦
ROM COM

NOVELLA

VIVIAN MAE

MIDTOWN PUBLISHING LLC

MERRY LITTLE
Mishap

"I CAN'T LEAVE YOU ALL LEAKY
AND WET, NOW. CAN I?"

TOO LATE, I THOUGHT.

Editor: The Romantic Editorial Services
Cover Art Illustrator: Sonia Garrigoux
Cover Design: Midtown Publishing LLC
First Edition: September 2023
Second Edition: October 2024
ISBN: 978-1-962659-03-1

Also By Vivian Mae

Standalone:

Burning Little Secrets

Merry Little Mishap

FREAK

Mine to Keep Series:

Lawsuit and Leather

Promise and Punishment

Dedication

To Mr. M.,
who's just as _handy_ as Nick Stafford.
Merry Christmas...

P.S. I'll take the pink Soraya Wave.
Thank you!
Your beloved, horny wife.

Playlists

Elena's playlist
1. Warm December - Sabrina Claudio
2. Tú - Maye
3. Moonlight - Kali Uchis
4. F.U.C.K. - Victoria Monét

Nick's playlist
1. Details - Leon Bridges
2. Holding On To Me - John Splithoff
3. Gimme Little Sign - Brenton Wood
4. Closer - Corinne Bailey Rae

Nick and Elena's playlist
1. I Just Melt - Sabrina Claudio
2. Do 4 Love - Snoh Aalegra
3. Moment - Victoria Monét
4. All for you - Amaria

Christmas Songs

1. This Christmas - Donny Hathaway
2. Santa Baby - Eartha Kitt
3. I'll Be Home For Christmas - Diana Krall
4. Have Yourself a Merry Little Christmas- Frank Sinatra

12 Reasons Nick
Stafford is the
Perfect Christmas Gift
EVER!!!
by Elena Ortiz

Reason #1

HE CARRIES A LARGE PACKAGE
Elena

When Nick Stafford brought the number two, best-selling dildo in the world to my door, I nearly died.

"Oh, Jesus!" I screamed—well sorta—it was more of a croak that shot out as I inhaled a screech that turned into a cough.

I tightened my fuzzy, pink robe, keeping it from flying open, eager to see Nick, but also berating myself for how ridiculous I looked: my hair dripping wet, falling into loose Puerto Rican curls that grazed my green, cucumber-melon face mask.

"Not Jesus, but Marty." Nick smiled. It was more of an apologetic grin that was as sincere as it was breathtaking. He nodded down to his German Shepard—Marty—who sat squinting at me with old gray whiskers. "He probably thought it was his Chewy subscription... they just keep giving me your mail on accident. Sorry about that."

"Well, you do live above me."

"622 does look a lot like 522," he winced, passing me the gnawed parcel with drool.

Quickly, I took it away, stuffing it underneath my pit, ignoring the hot-pink, silicon balls that poked out.

"It happens so often, we might as well just move in together." I smiled.

Then blinked.

Time suddenly stopped.

God, what the hell did I just say?

Somewhere, far from the old Prince Street apartment in Manhattan where I stood, Chrissy Teigen felt a cold December wind down her neck and cringed in my honor.

"And save me the pleasure of coming to your door? I don't think so, Elena." Nick said under his breath, his confidence as alarming as Marty's neon-green collar which rattled as he yawned.

That was Nick, though.

Hot, but cool.

Tempting, but intimidating, six feet and three inches of pure sun-kissed skin, and striking olive eyes. He slung his tool belt over his bicep, diverting his stare to the tips of his boots.

"I'm sure it's an inconvenience…" I fidgeted with my robe, double knotting it. He made me so nervous.

"Inconvenience is that sink of yours. Is it still on the fritz?"

"Leaking occasionally... but I put a bucket just below the—"

"Ah. No, no, no," he dismissed. "I'm the super... this is my job. I can't leave you all leaky and wet, now. Can I?"

Too late, I thought.

I stared again, ignoring the blatant awkwardness that followed his question. The masculine scent of his labor swirled with the juniper warmth of his faded cologne, comforting me with the most insatiable sense of tingles.

Only a second passed before I dropped my shoulders, my partially eaten package slipping from my arms.

Marty barked, as all nine inches of pornstar August Falls' molded penis tumbled to the floor, its base sticking to the glossy concrete with its vacuum-tight suction grip.

My skin melted below my face cream, burning red with a sudden sweat that took over my entire body.

Nick was always supremely cool, but me on the other hand, I was just as busted as the name smeared along the ruined postage on my package: Elena Maria Ortiz, the walking magnet of embarrassment to Nick Stafford. It had only been a year since I moved from San Juan, but he'd already caught me with lipstick on my teeth, my dress stuck on my panties, and now a dildo at my feet.

"I am *NOT* a sex freak!" I shouted, bending over, yanking the toy from the floor with a *pop*. "This isn't what you think. It's for work."

"It's fine."

"It's a lot to explain."

"Honestly you don't need to," he assured, chuckling.

I stuffed the dildo back into the box, on the verge of tears. I was always so painfully awkward, so self-conscious of every misstep as if the universe was hellbent on turning every interaction into a certain boobytrap.

"I'm sorry," I sighed.

"Sorry about what?"

"This... I'm so—"

"You're so kind... that's what you are," he interrupted. "You've been so patient with me... Hell, you've been patient with that god-awful sink in your kitchen. I know it's a hassle, especially in the midst of holiday chaos, and the last thing you need is me coming to your door and getting in your business..." His words slowed down, his voice mellow and deep as he peered down to meet my eyes. "I have time now, if you'd like me to come in?"

Nick.

My Christmas wish.

He was the saving grace to this old building; the man every single, and married, woman under this roof pined for, and he was much sweeter than any man I'd ever met. Yes, I felt like a fool around him, but I'd feel even more foolish if I didn't let him stay longer, hopelessly fantasizing about what we could never be.

"Of course, come in," I smiled, my dimples piercing my cheek. "Can I get you some coffee?"

Reason #2

He Knows How to Work a Pipe

Elena

"Cream, no sugar. Right?" I asked, remembering his coffee preference from the previous times he'd visited over the year.

"If it's not a bother." He cleared his throat, admiring my bright teal living room, my fake banana palms, and bohemian throws. "Love that you always keep those up." He nodded to the white string lights draped above my yellow couch.

"I'm thinking about keeping them up all year round! They really brighten up the place, right?"

"I'm not sure it could get any brighter. It's very cozy."

"Well, it's taken a while, but it's finally starting to feel like home... sorta." I shrugged, grabbing a nearby towel to wipe my face clean.

I walked into the kitchen, hiding my ruined

package in the pink cabinet next to a box of fruity pebbles. Hopefully, Nick wouldn't ask about it.

How could I explain that I was assigned my first paying gig with one of the biggest magazines in the world—*New York Prestige*—running a countdown list of the hottest sex toys of the season? *Twelve Days of Sex-Mas* had been as exhausting as it was thrilling, spending the last week getting off with various vibrators, Ben Wa balls, and butt plugs. I was surprised I was even walking straight at this point, and somehow calmly pouring Nick's cup of coffee.

"Honestly, I like the whole tropical vibe in here." Nick removed his denim jacket before lying down under the sink, chomping on a flashlight. His dark brown waves fell carelessly to his brows, his nose dimpled at the tip, mirroring the groove of his strong, peppered chin. "Marty won't even go outside to piss anymore... not without mittens. I'm ready to pack up and leave."

"Just don't go too far, who knows what else will break in this place? I *need* you."

"Who's to say I wouldn't take you with me? I'm sure you know all the best places for the warmest weather."

"Warmest beaches, too..." I inadvertently sipped his coffee, watching as his shirt lifted from his waist.

I tried really hard not to stare, fighting, resisting,

struggling with the temptation to gawk as he revealed a trail of trimmed hair on his firm torso. He cranked something underneath the sink, his arms tensing as he grunted.

"Name one for me."

"Name what?"

"A beach. Which one's your favorite?"

"Ah, *Playa Flamenco*. It's off the main island where I lived, but totally worth the trip if you can get a boat out there."

Nick hummed to himself.

"Playa Flamenco," he repeated my words. I couldn't see his face, but I could hear him smile. "How blue is the water?"

"Turquoise-clear... plenty of white sand, and warm sunlight."

Nick grew quiet, clanking a metal pipe.

"Sounds nice. But sounds even better coming from you." He noted my accent, my slight Caribbean-Spanish hitch. I combed a curl behind my ear, blushing. "Shit..."

"You ok?"

"Yes... it's just... the damn part I brought doesn't work."

"Again?"

"I'm so sorry, Elena." Nick lifted himself from the sink. "These pre-war buildings have some strange characteristics, and the plumbing is old as hell." He took the mug from my hand, taking a long sip of his coffee. I didn't mention I already drank from it and felt kinda guilty, but the way his broad shoulders dropped in relaxation was so rewarding. "I think I know what I need, but it will be about a week until it gets in. I was able to fix the leak, but it's only temporary."

He smiled.

I smiled back.

Everything grew quiet as I brushed my hair off to the side, twisting its ends with my red-painted nails. Nick tapped his mug before taking the last sip of coffee.

"Did you enjoy it?" I asked, desiring his praise.

"It hit the spot. Always does."

"If you liked that, then you'd love coquito. It's more of a holiday drink, though."

"Does it have chocolate?"

"Noooo," I waved away, taking his mug to rinse in the sink. I could feel him behind me, watching as I rambled on. "It's sorta like eggnog, but with condensed milk, cream of coconut, cinnamon..." I tried not to list everything, but then got excited, "Oh! And rum. Lots and lots of rum."

"Never heard of it."

I turned and huffed a curl out of my face, unable

to hide my grin. "It's more of a Puerto Rican thing. My family and I make it for Christmas every year, and believe me, after midnight mass in a very old, very stuffy church, a stiff drink was just what we needed. Unless, of course, you're my uncle Mateo. He's a priest."

"No booze for Father Mateo?" Nick leaned his elbow on the counter, making himself comfortable.

"Does the blood of Christ count?" I asked. "If so, then his cup runneth over. Besides that, I do recall him accidentally getting drunk from coquito one year while dipping his cup into a rum filled bowl at my family Christmas party. Everyone was gifted with extra blessings that night."

Nick cracked a smile as I ironically made the sign of the cross. He was always interested in my life back in Puerto Rico, enjoying the chaotic stories about my family with his uninterrupted gaze and attentive nod.

"They sound like a lot of fun." Nick shook his head, his hardy laugh rumbling from his chest. I loved that I could get that reaction from him, creased cheeks and eyes.

"They're the best. A little heavy on tradition. Marriage. Babies. Religious stuff... but I think their intentions are good."

We got quiet for a moment while I imagined a much worse scenario of my mami finding my sex toy as opposed to Nick. The shame would've been completely unbearable. That was one thing I didn't share with anyone—how the topic of sex was completely forbidden, a taboo of taboos that left my family in the dark over the countdown I was working on. They barely knew what I did for a living, my job description reduced to 'professional typist' for my abuelita to better understand.

Nick looked over at Marty, who sniffed under my empty Christmas tree. Not a single gift was placed beneath it, but the smell of pine wafted in our direction, not the least bit subdued by the smothering of lights and silver tinsel. Photos of my family decorated the branches, along with little colorful ornaments that I'd brought with me when I left home.

"And are you visiting your family for the holidays?"

Ugh. Please don't ask.

I was about to escape the purgatory of being an intern at New York Prestige, and this sex toy countdown I was working on meant my chances of being promoted to an associate editor were riding on this one silly assignment. I had no money to travel, let alone the desire to bring vibrators along to my *very* Catholic family gathering. Still, the fact that I couldn't go (that I couldn't make coquito on

Nochebuena—the biggest family event of the year), broke my heart.

"I, uh, decided to stay in New York this year." I kept it short. "You?"

"My sister in Jersey invited me over for dinner tonight."

"Fun!"

"Yeah, not really... it's nothing like your family parties, and between my nephews and the cousins involved, things tend to get a little overwhelming. Then there's my sister's ex-husband."

"He shows up, too?"

"Eh, yeah. They're cordial for the kids, but the tension is always suffocating," Nick mocked, wrapping his hand around his neck, his large, light eyes bright and hilariously worried. I giggled. "If there's anything I learned from those two, it's to never mix business with pleasure. She got involved with someone she worked with, and now they hate each other."

There was no hiding the look of dread on Nick's adorable, scruffy face. One Christmas was enough to last him an entire year, and had he been in Puerto Rico with his own family, he'd probably hang himself with garland at some point.

Christmas wasn't *just* a day back on the island.

No.

It was *La Navidad!*

Or as I saw it: a pants-tightening, food-devouring, forty-five day musical marathon with roasted pork.

Could Nick even fathom an entire month and a half filled with family gatherings and *parrandas?*

Wait.

Did they do *parrandas* here in the city? I think it's called 'caroling' in New York. I cringed, picturing how horrified Nick would look if his ex-brother-in-law lugged him around the middle of Times Square, caroling and strumming a guitar.

"Sounds like fun," I said.

"Fun is doing your taxes. I'm looking for any excuse not to go." Nick's eyes wandered around again, following his brief silence. He focused down at a stack of *New York Prestige* magazines, their pages noted with colorful sticky tabs. "Fan of the magazine?"

"For work," I shrugged, organizing the various pamphlets from my favorite Chinese restaurant. He picked up the menu, reading its red logo—*Sichuan Garden.*

"You work for New York Prestige?"

"Currently. Just something small for now but trying to move up."

Nick placed the menu back down on the counter, nodding his classic little approval that I adored. "Lots of pretty girls there," he said, staring into my eyes, but I diverted away to the gorgeous model on the cover.

Yes, lots of pretty girls—girls who didn't look like me, because honestly, since working there not many people did. I wasn't the tall, five-foot-eleven blonde, with large breasts and designer handbags. Instead, I was petite, built with a small waist, large hips, and an ass like a peach; some compact woman with long, black, curly hair and small breasts. According to the magazines I wasn't the pretty girl, and since coming here, I started to believe it.

"*Yeah... lots,*" I parroted.

"Well, I have particular taste in women." Nick flipped the magazine over, placing its cover face down. "I hope I didn't take too long. I'm sure you have plans tonight. You look like you're getting ready for something."

God! I was getting ready, and suddenly I felt so shy about why. Going to my holiday office party wasn't a big deal, though the fact that I had a plus-one ticket to give away was. Nick was essentially begging for an excuse to leave his family gathering, and here I had the perfect solution to solve his problem.

I watched Marty, who undoubtedly sniffed around for the dildo, waiting patiently below the cabinet I stored it in.

I tried not to clench my teeth and scream.

The truth was I was nowhere near Nick's league. He was a ten, a solid—muscle-wrapped, Calvin Klein model—ten. And I... I was the epitome of an unpolished shrew. Despite working for *New York Prestige,* I wasn't your typical *New York Prestige* girl, and I certainly lacked the confidence of one. Regardless, there was still one absolute truth that I held close to my heart: that I could survive the constant awkward moments I shared with Nick, but in turn, would never be able to survive his rejection. *It would kill me.*

I froze.

"No plans tonight... just pulling an all-nighter for a deadline I have. Work, work, work," I snorted, trying not to flail my arms, stewing in the awful lie I told to an otherwise disappointed Nick Stafford.

Reason #3

HE'S SMOKING HOT

Nick

"Do you like blondes, redheads or brunettes?" Mrs. Caporali asked from the kitchen, wiping her hands clean of flour.

Marty circled around her as she carried a new tray of sugar cookies from the oven to a cooling rack. Being that the apartment was no bigger than a matchbox, I was able to keep eyes on my mischievous old pup, my ears like sonar to his jostling collar.

"Brunettes. I'm a total sucker for them," I answered from her bathroom, screwdriver clenched between my teeth.

She gasped.

She always gasps.

"I have eleven granddaughters just for you!" She clapped her hands together, her glasses slipping down her nose. "Each is a varying shade of brunette.

I have dark brown, honey brown, chestnut, auburn, toffee, caramel..."

Marty finally sat in front of the oven, hopelessly staring through the little, dark window that blocked him from the fresh batch of raw cookie dough that Mrs. Caporali just tossed in. How many batches had she planned on baking, anyway? She already force fed me three; the green frosting and sprinkles caked on my tongue.

"Brilliant bronze, milk chocolate, savory pecan, cedar...?" she pointed to Marty's paws as visual comparison.

"How about dark espresso?" I interrupted, balancing on a ladder to fix her broken smoke detector—her third one this year.

"How dark are we talking?"

Jingle Bells bounced over the radio, filling the space to her unanswered question.

I thought about it for a moment, carefully considering the answer, because I took it very seriously.

How could I explain to Mrs. Caporali that her granddaughters' hair couldn't be darker, or lighter, than the girl who lived next door to her apartment?

How could I even articulate that?

How, without a stutter in my voice, could I share that the perfect shade of color was second to the cheeks it rested on, or the cute little ears it laid over, or the very head it grew from?

God, even the word *espresso* as a descriptor was so unfitting—worthy of being kindle to a fireplace—because the color itself could only be encompassed with something as unique as the person it belonged to.

Elena Ortiz.

The back of my neck dripped in sweat just from the thought of her, and admitting that to someone as gossipy as Mrs. Caporali would be a total nightmare for me as a professional in this building.

"Her hair needs to be dark. Obsidian and shiny. Silky and curly," I finally said, twisting wires together.

"Curly?" She announced with surprise, digging her hands into the pockets of her red apron.

She rocked back and forth on her heels, flipping through some mental rolodex where she stored all her granddaughters.

My phone rang in my tool belt, saving me from her impending elevator speech.

"One moment," I said to Mrs. Caporali before answering my phone. "Hello?"

"If you get me anything for Christmas this year, please let it be a genie lamp..." Tiffany, my older sister sighed through the phone, her voice rushed as always. "I'm ready to wish Hank away! Can someone —*anyone*—please just send that man back to whatever polo-wearing, golf-club-swinging, Viagra-using *HELL* he crawled out of?! Did I tell you he got the promotion over me? Me, Nick! *Me!* Can you believe that?"

"You mean your ex-husband—the man who originally hired you for your current job—got a better position at the same company you both work at?"

This was the third time she told me about the promotion. At this point my ear was just a punching bag for her rage filled rants. She hated her ex-husband so damn much.

"He's going bald, you know... I *love* it," she said with as much Christmas glee as she could muster, before something crashed on the other end of the phone. "BOYS! What did I tell you about bikes in the house? Only at your father's!"

I tried really hard not to groan.

"I'm guessing Santa came early this year?"

"Hank surprised them like some hot shot. I hope he burns his tongue on hot cocoa. Boys, say *hi* to your uncle Nicky."

A myriad of shouts and bike brakes screeched through the line.

I pulled the phone away from my ear momentarily.

"They're excited to see you tonight," she muffled.

Something *popped* on Tiffany's side.

"What's that noise?" I asked.

"What noise?" she slurped.

"Are you drinking wine right now?"

"Just a light moscato. Something to soothe the headaches. *BOYS!*"

I dropped my phone, and it tumbled to the floor.

Marty barked.

"How about wavy?" Mrs. Caporali asked, sucking on a sharpened, peppermint candy cane. "My granddaughter, Dorothea, has *very* wavy hair. In fact, I'd consider it curly."

"Seems like a stretch if I'm being honest." I arched a brow.

Mrs. Caporali was as cunning as a used car salesman, but as patient as a monk. You'd think after two years of trying to persuade me on this that she'd give up by now. I was such an idiot to think that.

"She's stacked, you know..." Mrs. Caporali picked up my phone, eyebrows wiggling. "You could use her bosoms as a shelf for your tools! She's got a great pair for all your future babies." She demonstrated, her hands held out, cradling the weight of imaginary double-Ds.

My eyes widened.

"That's good to know..." I took my phone back,

blowing powdered sugar off the screen. "I have a lot of tools though. Let me think about your proposal."

Was she serious?

The last thing on my mind was babies, especially with my nephews screaming on the other end of my sister's call.

"Who was that?" Tiffany asked.

"A tenant," I whispered. "I think she keeps breaking her smoke detectors to get me over to her house. She's not even hiding the evidence anymore. The hammer she used to smash the last one is still in the bathroom sink."

"She must have the hots for you." Tiffany snickered.

My nephews oohed and whistled behind her.

"I think she's trying to pawn me off to her granddaughters... A harem for the holidays."

"Oh... gross!" she echoed into her wine glass. "Listen. Can you bring some dinner for the boys tonight?"

"Dinner? Wait... I thought you were making a ham?"

"Plans changed."

"How so?"

"Hank's bringing that blonde bimbo, Barbara, over for Christmas dinner."

Oh, god. Not Bimbo Barbara.

My heart sank at her tone. I was already dreading this evening.

"Why don't you tell him no, Tiff?" I suggested kindly.

She didn't take it well.

"You can't be serious!"

"Why not?"

Tiffany took a long breath.

"And how would I say that without sounding totally scorned, Nicky? Like... *no Hank, you can't bring that tapered waisted floozy you cheated on me with to our family dinner, you scumbag.*"

Marty's ears perked from Tiffany's voice.

I nodded approvingly.

"Your wording is a little harsh, but I think he'd get the point."

Tiffany disagreed.

"Listen, I'm not giving that man the satisfaction of knowing I'm upset." The sound of wine poured through the phone, followed by chugging. "This is a moment to show off my killer culinary skills, something *his* tits with legs probably doesn't know a thing about. We're having bacon-wrapped tenderloins with mushroom chutney."

"Mushroom *what?*"

"Ch-ut-ney..." she repeated slowly. "Don't worry. It's delicious. But the boys are gagging at it. Nick, you know I can't have Hank bring his secretary, slash, blowup-doll here without me trying to show off how happy I am without him. Even though that's not true. God... I just hate seeing the two of them together at work."

Tiffany's dreaded office romance plagued every family gathering since they split up three years ago. It wasn't just messy, it was a relentless tug-of-war that pinned my nephews in an all-out battle over whose affection could be won first.

Could you imagine if I ever made the same mistake?

Sure, I didn't work with anyone in the building, but the tenants were essentially my customers. I saw them every day, sometimes multiple times in a single day.

Marty barked at the oven, tail swishing back and forth on the floor. I gave him a quick *shush*.

He was already in trouble after this morning, and damn it, I couldn't believe he actually chewed up Elena's package today.

No. Not just chewed it up... but soaked the damn box with all his slobber! My palms started to sweat the moment I saw those pink balls slipping out of her sticky parcel, my heart beating double time when I pried it out of Marty's growling mouth in a fit of panic. Shit... actually, it wasn't just my palms that sweat, but my temples and nose, too.

Had Elena noticed the embarrassing amount of collected beads running across my forehead, dripping down onto her wooden floors? Okay, maybe it wasn't that bad, but my mind conjured up a much crueler memory than what most likely happened.

My face felt so flushed just thinking of it, my stomach a warm pool of adrenaline that swirled at the thought of Elena ever playing with that inadequate pink dildo.

Was it wrong that I found it so incredibly hot that she had a sex toy shipped to her house? She made it clear that it was just for work—whatever that meant—but that didn't stop me from imagining all the ways she'd use it; moaning in her wrought iron bed, her thighs spread open with her panties yanked down to her ankles.

Did she like it fast?

Slow?

I ran my fingers through my hair, trying to get ahold of my senses, but was overwhelmed with the thought of Elena's perfect little tits, shaking in an orgasm, her back on that cute yellow couch of hers—a couch I wanted to pull her down into and kiss her just how Mrs. Caporali probably wanted me to kiss one of her granddaughters.

I'd kill for that moment.

I'd kill for less!

I'd take Elena right into my mouth, and bite that sweet, puffy—

"You like em' tan, don't you?" Mrs. Caporali popped up again, my ladder rattling from how hard she made me jump.

"Jesus!"

"Dorothea is fair-skinned. Is that a deal breaker?" she asked, her hand cupped over a phone, cord stretching all the way back to the kitchen. Marty was tangled in it.

"Are you talking to your granddaughter right now?" I asked, bewildered.

"I have her on hold. She can get a spray tan by twelve if you want to come over for dinner at seven?"

"Tell her you already have plans!" Tiffany panicked on the other line. I'd forgotten she was on the phone, because all I could think about was Elena.

I hated being pulled in every-which-way, my nephews screaming, Tiffany cussing over spilt wine, and Mrs. Caporali looking up with hopeful eyes.

It was pure insanity.

And to make it worse, despite all these invitations, a part of me felt guilty, because I wanted none of them.

I had all these people around me, but the only

one I wanted was the girl next door who was alone for Christmas.

What the hell was that about?

Why wasn't someone by her side at all times? Holding her. Celebrating with her. Kissing her under mistletoe and drinking coquito.

Why couldn't that be me?

I already knew why...

"Nick!" Tiffany shouted over the phone.

"Yes! I'll pick up food for the kids..."

"Great! Oh, god... Hank's here, I have to go. Bring wine. LOTS of wine!"

Tiffany hung up, but Mrs. Caporali still had her granddaughter on the phone.

"Well?" she asked.

I rolled my eyes to the ceiling so she wouldn't see.

"Mrs. Caporali..."

"Call me Beatrice. I'm practically your future grandmother-in-law."

I took a deep breath and smiled. *Very nicely.*

"Beatrice... I'm sorry, but I have dinner plans tonight. And for the record, I like a woman who's short, tan, has dark curly hair and bright brown, beautiful eyes..."

Mrs. Caporali—Beatrice—rested her elbow on the ladder, her candy cane stuck back into her mouth like a cigar.

I could tell she was contemplating.

"Well, hell. You should just date that cute lil' Puerto Rican girl next door!"

Just then, from the other side of Beatrice's bathroom wall, the sound of shower water sputtered into life—Elena's shower specifically.

This building was so old, so thin with ancient bricks, that every audible creaky pipe could be heard with ease. I plastered my eyes right onto the wall, knowing only feet away Elena was naked.

First, I felt like some pervert, unable to stop myself from imagining Elena Ortiz covered in slippery wet suds. She was so fucking beautiful.

Second, I felt like a total asshole, because the truth was, I could've fixed her sink weeks ago.

What the hell was I even doing?

I knew it was wrong, but I needed any excuse to keep seeing her again—to be around her—to hear her accent, to drink her coffee and, god... to smell that peach, pineapple spray she wore anytime she answered the door.

She was a thousand miles away from any family, and damn it, a pathetic part of me wanted to give her even the tiniest slice of what she might've been missing back in Puerto Rico.

Truth was, I wanted to break the pattern of

holiday chaos. I wanted a new tradition. I wanted Elena...

Could the same be true for her?

Don't be stupid, Nick. Think of Tiffany and Hank.

I cringed.

If it was one thing I knew, it was that falling for someone you worked around would never end well.

"I don't think that would be a good idea," I finally answered Mrs. Caporali, my final words punctuated by the screeching smoke detector I just installed.

Reason #4

He's Easily Likable

Elena

"You're telling me that Henry Cavill could have been here tonight, and you didn't invite him?" Camilla Martinez, my boss and staff writer at *New York Prestige* gasped as she stared at my phone. I tried to steal it back, but her manicured, cranberry nails swiped feverishly across Nick's Instagram feed.

"He's hotter than Henry," I defended, the almost sacrilegious statement for who she compared him to.

It was true though, Nick was hotter; a little older than me—probably mid-thirties—a tad larger in the forearms than Henry, and with just as deep of a voice.

"Sure, he's not superman, but he might as well be." I sipped on my third Mistletoe Martini, trying to dance as little as possible as a jazz pianist played *Santa Baby* in the corner. The music, the chatter, and the massive fifteen-foot Christmas tree that sat center of the lobby were all enriched by the soft, Manhattan snow that sauntered across our skyscraper view of Madison Avenue and 42nd Street.

"Well, he's definitely a hero, or better yet, the man of my dreams." Camilla oohed and awed, flipping the phone over, showing me the screen occasionally. On it, Nick carried a case of new tennis balls to an animal shelter, Marty barking by his side. "Did you see his vinyl collection? Oh, and he makes his own pizzas?"

"He fixes everything in the building, too. He's good with his hands."

"*Oh*, I'm sure he is." Camilla peered over the table-top candle, her large, black eyes caught in the flame. "And wait... he saw your dildo?"

"God, don't remind me." I pinched the bridge of my nose, my cheeks hot from embarrassment and strong vodka.

"Relax, amiga. He's obviously cool about it."

"Ok, yeah, but that doesn't excuse the fact that he's always catching me in the worst situations."

"But he still comes over, doesn't he?"

"He has to, he's my super."

"But nobody is making him drink your coffee. Coffee's a date."

"Coffee's a courtesy. It's hospitality."

"This day and age, coffee is the precursor to dinner, which is also the precursor to moving in and splitting the rent. You're practically twelve months away from getting engaged." Camilla reached up, fixing my antler headband with the flick of its little jingle bells. I tried not to roll my eyes, the thought of ever marrying Nick, let alone being on a date with him felt so unreal.

I tugged on my black turtleneck, feeling antsy as I adjusted the length of my plaid skirt. Nick was clearly into models, which meant at least half the staff here was his type, but not me. Even Camilla, the only other Latina in the building, was different than me. She was taller, her hair flat and sleek, her breasts fuller, and her hips more trimmed. She was devastatingly gorgeous in her luscious black, floor-length gown, shimmering gold earrings, and thin see-through stilettos. She didn't have to even resemble Christmas, because she lit up the entire room with her radiant smile. If only I could have an ounce of that confidence.

"He said he has *particular* taste." I took another long sip of my Martini, catching Camilla's attention.

"Yeah... *particularly* for a twenty-five-year-old Puerto Rican," she laughed as if I were being stubborn and foolish.

"No."

"Uh, *yes*."

"He likes magazine hotties."

"You *are* a magazine hottie."

"Yeah, maybe for *Highlights Magazine*. I feel like a girl amongst women out here."

"I see what you mean." Camilla gave me some playful side-eye.

"So, you agree?"

"I do. But not for the reason you think. You're gorgeous, trust me, and you don't need to be some amazonian blonde to be desired. You need confidence! That's what's sexy, that's what's attractive." Camilla tucked a strand of my hair back into my ponytail. "Honestly, I'd kill for these curls; I know Nick would, too."

"You've had too much Jingle Juice," I scoffed.

"It's true! Your hair is to die for! Your lips are real, your smile is white, your skin is glowing like Rockefeller Center."

"Ok, now I know you're drunk."

"Maybe, but so are you. And what you need is a Christmas angel to give you a little push." Camilla swiped at my phone once more, double tapping not one, but three of Nick's photos. The little red hearts popped on the screen, showing that I *liked* his posts.

I wasn't even following his account.

"Camilla!" I screeched, snatching my phone out of her hands.

She cackled. "Don't unlike them either. It'll be more awkward if you do."

"I can't believe you." I tossed back the last of my drink, stuffing my phone back into my purse.

"Believe it. And that's not the only gift I'm giving you." She reached into her bag, pulling out a carefully wrapped box with a large red bow.

"Awe, you didn't have to get me anything!"

"Well, it's actually the last item for your countdown. I've been keeping my eye on your posts, and they're a massive hit on instagram."

"They've been a big hit for my personal life, too. As long as this one doesn't get chewed up by Marty."

"Actually, this one is meant to be shared… but no dogs for Christ's sake. Maybe Nick can help you open it."

"Ugh… I need another drink." I slid my arms into my matching plaid blazer, fixing the gold hoops in my ears.

"Remember… it's all about confidence. I know from experience. My ugliest moments are when I'm most insecure… it's not me, it's my fear." Camilla gave me a quick hug. "Now, don't forget. Finish up this last review, and I'll promote you to associate editor. You'll officially be on the payroll."

We said our goodbyes one final time before I turned away, package in hand, and a pep talk that felt more like a cheer up, than an actual plan I could ever pull off.

Reason #5

He Doesn't Keep
Things Bottled Up

Nick

Across Washington Square Park, below bushy green garland and white string lights was O'Malley's hand painted sign; a once old Irish pub now turned liquor store.

"You could at least get rid of the menu that's still hanging in the window." I brushed Manhattan snow off my shoulder, shivering in my topcoat as I climbed the warm steps into the entrance.

"I like the charm of it, besides, nobody would actually go to a pub to eat. It's all about the spirits, *mi mano*." Luis greeted, wiping down the original sticky bar top.

I laughed and nodded around, lifting a twelve-year-old bottle of WhistlePig from one of the built-in mahogany shelves.

Outside of the missing barstools and newly added Dominican flags, this place stayed completely untouched from how it used to look; its intricately carved banisters and dark crown molding aged by the wear and tear of generations that had traversed its chestnut floors for over a century.

Even Luis knew it'd be criminal to ever remove the hanging Tiffany lights that were strung about, their warm glow casting perfect cozy shadows along the copper tiled ceiling and forest green wallpaper.

"Let me guess, Marty's driving you to drink again?" Luis leaned on the counter, scratching his mustache. "Or did the ol' pooch send you on an errand for himself? I'm guessing he's a peppermint schnapps kind of dog."

I shopped around and shook my head. "I'm actually here for my *very* thirsty sister. You wouldn't happen to have a barrel of wine handy, would you?"

Luis whistled, "How about a box of it?"

"I'm sure anything with a handle would suffice."

"I second that." A customer in the whiskey section added, dragging his freshly cut Christmas tree across the floor to the counter. His face was stricken with holiday horror. "I just spent two hundred dollars on *this* Nobel Fir... *TWO HUNDRED*. All because *my* insufferable mother-in-law *had* to have it!" He stomped the tree trunk onto the floor, gritting his teeth. "Well, guess what lady...

you may *need* this overpriced fire hazard, but *I* need a stiff drink just to make it through the holidays with you! Believe me when I say, I'd much sooner dress like an angel and sit on top of this tree than have *you* ruin the single drink I waited for all year long. So help me god, I'll have my eggnog how I like it, even if *you* say it spoils my breath!" he announced loudly, as if rehearsing before his final performance.

Luis quickly bagged a bottle for the man, sympathetically punching numbers into the cash register before wishing him a Merry Christmas.

The bell at the door chimed as he exited, trudging out into the street with his tree.

We both got quiet and stared at each other.

"*Feliz Navidad*, Nick!" Angela, Luis's wife, greeted me as she made her way from the cellar, bags of heavy bottles in hand. "Are you here to pick something up for Marty?"

"Why does everyone think my dog's an alcoholic?" I arched a brow, concerned about his reputation. "I'm actually here for my sister."

"Tiffany?" she asked, yanking a receipt from the register, stapling it onto the bags.

Luis and Angela seriously know way too much about my life.

"She wants wine, but I'm guessing she needs

something much stronger," Luis added, side eyeing the TV mounted in the corner of the bar. *It's a Wonderful Life* flickered on the screen.

"I think she'd settle for horse tranquilizers if you have any," I muttered, arbitrarily lifting bottles and putting them back down.

I didn't know why I was so sheepish, but I hesitated reaching into my coat pocket, removing the piece of folded paper I brought from home.

Carefully, I opened it up, keeping it close to my chest.

"One can of condensed milk... one can of evaporated milk... cream of coconut... half cup white rum." I said under my breath, studying it while moving to the rum section.

I obsessively searched online for an authentic coquito recipe after leaving Mrs. Caporali's this afternoon, because I just couldn't shake how Elena's face lit up when she shared a little piece of her holiday tradition with me.

My face hurt from grinning, my rosy cheeks heated like a crush stricken middle schooler.

What was this spell Elena had over me? This ability to make me melt in the middle of a liquor store aisle, to turn every moment we shared into an impossible task of keeping my hands to myself.

I replayed her day-defining, mood-lifting smile in

my head, my memory like a delicate sketch artist to her cherry blossom lip gloss. I couldn't get over her beautiful apple cheeks, her addicting laugh like a drug I desperately wanted all to myself. Hell, that pretty face of hers, matched with her incredible soul was the very reason I spent hours searching online for the perfect coquito recipe, writing it down, checking it twice.

And no... just because I scoured the internet for this invaluable concoction, didn't mean I was actually going to do anything about it.

"Valuing Elena's interest isn't wrong... nor does looking for the ingredients to her favorite holiday drink mean I'm headed towards some romantic downfall," I told myself, fearing the inevitable tipping point that would spiral me into some chain of relationship failure like my sister. I cleared my throat. "Luis... what would you consider to be a good choice of white rum?"

"Depends. What's it being used for? Piña Colada? Mojito? Cajun Lemonade?"

"No. None of that."

"Is it for a strawberry daiquiri?"

I scratched at my chin. Why was I being so weird?

Luis made his way from behind the counter to the rum rack where I stood, sighing. "Don't get too specific and bore me with the details," he said, amused.

Christ. My hands got so stuffy in my leather gloves.

Luis looked down at the paper.

"Coquito?" He nodded approvingly, a shot of realization washing over his face. "We have lots of options for that. Bacardi, Don Q... Havana Club is a good one. Distilled in Puerto Rico."

"Puerto Rico?!" I gasped, instinctually reaching out and taking it. Why did it feel like I had the world's greatest treasure in my hand?

Elena would like this one. I held onto it like it was the last life vest on a sinking ship.

"What about the wine?" Luis pointed to the other side of the store.

Wine? I didn't care about wine at all right now. All I cared about was how this little bottle of rum made my heart skip. My intentions of coming here were totally hijacked with the desire to grab everything I needed for Elena's favorite seasonal drink.

"Do you know what Tiffany's wanting?" Luis asked again, taking the bottle of rum from my hand so I could shop easier.

He had to pry it away.

"Damn. I really don't know." I patted my pockets

for my phone but felt nothing. "I left my cell back home."

"You can use ours if you want?" Angela pulled out an old rotary phone from behind the bar, setting it next to the register with a loud thump. She grunted from the weight. "Try and keep it domestic."

"No promises... I'm pretty sure New Jersey is considered its own country at this point." I checked my watch, realizing how far I had to travel still. From this point it'd take me well over an hour to get to Tiffany's.

Patiently, I dialed her number, spinning my finger on the janky rotary wheel, waiting for it to reset after each digit. The phone rang and rang.

I braced for the noise.

"Hello!" Tiffany finally answered, my nephews once again shouting in the background, along with cousins, uncles and aunts.

"Tiff, it's Nick."

"Nick... please tell me you're just around the corner."

She was going to kill me.

"I will be..." I hesitated, hoping she could hear my smile, "in just about... an hour and forty minutes."

"Nicky!" she screamed.

"Relax, relax. I'm getting your prescription wine.

I just need to know exactly what you want." I slid my coquito recipe across the bar top, pointing to the ingredients. *"Do you have condensed milk?"* I mouthed to Luis, and he nodded, taking my list in hand.

"What about dinner for the boys? They're starving!" Tiffany said.

"I already ordered them pizza before leaving my apartment. Two boxes of piping hot pepperoni are headed their way. Extra cheese."

Luis came back to the register, piling cans of ingredients next to my rum.

"Could you call them back and order three more boxes? I sorta burned my tenderloins."

"She nuked them!" Hank—Tiffany's awful ex—barked behind her, his husky cackle carrying into my receiver.

I massaged the headache in my eyes, holding the phone away as they argued over the definition of *nuked.*

The brass bell at the entrance chimed, and a gusty winter wind rolled towards my feet.

"There's a guy out front who needs help tying his Christmas tree to his car." A shivering delivery man announced, walking up to the register with his bike helmet still on.

Luis and I looked out the window, watching as

his customer from earlier windmilled his arms before slipping on black ice. His ass hit the floor, and his tree rolled off the roof of his car and into a gutter.

The delivery man paid no attention, unzipping his backpack to pull out a bag of food.

"Sichuan Garden?" I gasped, unexpectedly surprised by its bright red letters and swirling long dragon.

What were the chances of seeing this now? Right in the middle of getting ingredients for coquito.

Elena had a takeout menu for this *very* same place on her kitchen counter this morning, and now, I was smelling the most delicious sweet and sour scent from a bag with its logo on it.

It felt like the universe was tapping my shoulder.

"Do you have a menu?" I asked the delivery guy, taking it from his hand while uncapping a red pen next to Luis's register.

Hypothetically... if I were to *ever* pick up food for Elena, what would she even like?

"Their egg rolls are my favorite. Plus, their wontons taste like the crispy *yaniqueque* my mom used to make." Luis split his chopsticks, rubbing them together.

"Taste like what?" I asked, circling the wontons on the menu.

"It's a Dominican thing. Have you ever had fried

dough? Never mind. The important thing is that it tastes like home."

I scratched under my chin, sitting with Luis's words that somehow struck a chord in my heart.

Like home, he said.

Home was what I wanted Elena to feel like, and damn... I knew Elena liked Sichuan Garden, but savory Chinese food wasn't exactly the staple of a Puerto Rican Christmas dinner. Could it be a decent substitute?

I chewed on the end of the pen, thinking about what else she'd like, deciding to circle both the chow mein and sesame chicken.

"How's the shrimp?" I asked Luis, ignoring Tiffany as she continued to argue with Hank.

"It's my favorite," Angela added, bringing me a few sticks of cinnamon for the coquito.

The delivery man nodded in agreeance.

I circled the shrimp twice.

"Nicky!" Tiffany finally got back on the line, her background less hectic.

"I'm still here," I answered, writing out the imaginary details to my hypothetical dinner with Elena. *I wonder if she'd like fried rice?*

"Scrap the wine. Bring me whatever they gave The Civil War soldiers before amputating legs." I could hear Tiffany fall into a bed, either her own or one of the kids.

"I'm not sure if they have any chloroform here..."

"A pillow over the face will suffice." She let out a sigh.

"Sounds like you've stepped away from the party," I muttered, watching as the man outside finally gave up, tossing his Christmas tree into his trunk, slamming half of it shut. Pine needles exploded everywhere.

"I'm in the boys' room right now."

"Napping?"

"I'm hiding chocolate bars in their pillowcases. I'm going to tell them it's reindeer poop." Tiffany cracked a smile.

I chuckled, knowing my nephews would love that. They had exceptional humor.

We were quiet for a moment, and I watched as Luis fed Angela a piece of crispy honey chicken.

They laughed.

They kissed.

They'd been married for longer than I'd existed, and they worked harmoniously in a liquor store together. But if boozy holiday drinks were the secret to long term love, then it sure as hell didn't work for Tiffany and Hank.

"I have a headache," Tiffany admitted with a groggy voice.

I hesitated.

"How about I bring you some water instead?" I asked, half joking, half serious. There was no doubt in my mind she already finished the bottle of moscato from earlier.

"Water is good," she yawned.

"Do you still want me to order more pizza?"

"Mmmm..." she muttered undecidedly.

She went quiet.

"Tiffany?"

More silence.

"Tiff?" I asked.

What the hell happened to her? All I heard was ambient room noises, followed by the most obnoxious snore.

God, she fell asleep!

"Tiffany, are you serious right now!" After a few more moments of calling her name, I finally hung up.

Resting my elbow on the bar, I looked at the pile of ingredients for coquito and a Chinese takeout menu scribbled with indecisive choices for a dinner I wish I could have, but was afraid would lead to inevitable disappointment.

I watched as Luis wiped wonton crumbs off Angela's cheek, unsure if my fear of ending up like

Tiffany was even valid anymore. I was wrecked, my mind and heart an endless, revolving carousel of Elena's beautiful face.

"How have you both stayed married for so long without it ending badly?" I asked. They were both surprised by the impromptu question.

They looked at each other, then averted their attention to the man outside punching his Christmas tree.

Luis and Angela came to some silent agreement and shrugged. "You have to find the person you want to drink *with*... not the person you have to drink *because* of."

The crunch of an egg roll ended the most succinct piece of advice I'd ever heard.

I opened my mouth. Then shut it.

I felt like I'd been an idiot this whole time, dumbstruck by Luis's casual liquor store advice. I stared down at the rotary phone, at the pile of coquito ingredients, and the Sichuan Garden menu.

I was headed this direction all along, but I was just too stubborn to go after what I actually wanted this Christmas.

I knew the risk.

I knew the reward.

And while Tiffany fell asleep in my nephew's bed, and the man outside drove away (not realizing his tree had fallen out of the trunk), I lifted the rotary phone blindly, and let my heart take control with each spin of the numbers until the phone started to ring.

There was no going back now.

"Hello? Sichuan Garden? I'd like to place an order to go..."

Reason #6

He Comes With the Best Type of Baggage

Elena

I couldn't believe Camilla, my personal romantic assassin, liking the most random posts on Nick's Instagram feed. Like it were a car wreck, I couldn't help but stare, recoiling at the illuminated heart that sat below a photo of Nick holding a Donny Hathaway album from years ago. *Years!*

"Aww Jesus," I whispered to myself, shivering in the dim lobby of my apartment complex, smashing the elevator button once again. I had one goal, and one goal alone; get upstairs, avoid Nick at all costs, and enjoy the Martini-induced deep sleep that I earned.

I leaned against a row of mailboxes, tucked in the corner as the front lobby door swung open.

I fought from groaning, peeking up from my phone whose low battery logo flashed on my screen.

Dear god, don't do this...

Nick-fucking-Stafford walked through the large, windowed door, his face stern from the cold wind outside, but it softened as he made eyes at me.

"Nick!" I smiled, crossing one leg over the other, letting out the most god-awful chortle. *Why am I this way?* I tried not to stumble, my holiday drinks already making their way down to my wobbly posture.

"Elena?" he said surprised, scanning me up and down, assessing me, my outfit, my face. "I, uh... thought you..." he shook his head, stopping his thought. "How are you?"

"I'm god," I said, shutting my eyes. "*Good.* I mean, I'm good."

Silence followed as Nick shifted his weight. He muscled over large plastic bags from one hand to the other, balancing a paper grocery sack between his bicep and chest. I watched as he carefully bit down on the tip of his black leather gloves, snatching them free, letting them loose into the bag before licking his lips.

"Still have that deadline tonight?"

"Yes." I peered over Camilla's carefully wrapped package that rested on the floor. "Actually, I have more to do than I thought. It's going to be a busy night."

"It's already pretty late, isn't it?"

I nodded, checking how his black chinos and boots matched perfectly with his long topcoat and heather-gray sweater. I appreciated how long his hair started to become, his duck tails swooped back into perfect waves. He was dressed nice, neat even, a sobering contrast to his equally sexy, rugged, morning look from earlier.

The elevator door opened up as Nick gestured for me to go first. I hurried awkwardly, lifting Camilla's present into my arms, entering. Somehow inside felt even quieter, as we both reached for the same button. What a gentlemen, pressing my level before his. We each pulled back and laughed.

God. More silence and accidental eye gazing.

Was he thinking about me *liking* his posts? Had he seen it already? I wondered, suddenly feeling too warm as I unbuttoned my coat.

"No family party tonight?" I finally asked, the elevator creaking in the background.

Nick smiled to himself. "I kind of bailed on that."

"Not in the mood?"

"Not exactly. I love my sister, love my nephews... just wanted to try something different tonight."

"Like compete in an eating contest?" I joked, noticing the familiar *Sichuan Garden* logo on his plastic bags. He looked to be carrying nearly ten pounds of my favorite Chinese food.

"Thought I would give it a try... besides, Marty loves the leftovers."

"He seems like a chow-mien kinda dog."

"Think more broccoli and beef." Nick tilted his head, his eyes shifting. He suddenly seemed so self-conscious of the bags, staring at them, his face washed with indifference.

He reached for the pocket in his jacket, for what I assumed was his phone.

I panicked, my stomach instantly twisting into a knot.

This was it; he was going to see the notifications now if he hadn't already.

"I didn't mean to like your posts!" I blurted out, leaning against the railing of the elevator wall.

Nick pulled out a piece of gum from his pocket, sticking it into his mouth. He chewed, just letting my random statement float around with no response.

"What posts?" he asked curiously, almost confused.

"Oh..."

"You liked one of my posts? Like on Instagram?"

"Well, a friend did... I mean I like them, too, but..."

"So, you were with a friend?" Nick scanned me once more, but this time his gaze lingered much longer on my lips. I wasn't sure if he was relieved or concerned.

"She's my boss... it's complicated."

"Hmmm," Nick sighed. "I thought for some reason you were on a date."

"Date?" I snorted, smoothing over my hair, its taut texture blooming into curls on the other end of my ponytail. "No. No date. Never a date."

"Never?"

Don't make me relive this.

I faked a smile.

"The last one I went on ended with an awkward handshake turned fist bump."

Nick shook his head, "That's terrible."

"I know, right! Anyway, safe to say, it didn't work out. Since then, it's been crickets in the dating department."

"I don't believe that," he said, rather confidently. "Especially tonight, I can't imagine you going out like that... and not being hit on."

"Like what?" I stared down at my outfit, playing with its gold buttons.

"Like that, Elena..." he rolled his eyes, amused. "It's just that you look nice... like, *really, really,* nice."

Nick stared for a hard second, which turned into two, then three. My head swirled with blood and booze, my lips numb to a buzz that surely made me blush.

Me? Nice looking?

His determination to not look away was met with the most alluring challenge, as Camilla's daunting cackle morphed into an encouraging chant in my head.

Do it, do it, do it!

I squeezed onto the gift, the elevator beeping loudly, stilling time as my mouth opened and my breath fell short into the most confident response I could muster.

I wasn't sure how I did it, or why it suddenly felt so easy, but my words spilled out in perfect harmony to the unapologetic sincerity of my eyes.

"You look good, too, Nick." I twisted my hands, trying to, but unable to resist the most obnoxious smile. "Actually, I think you're really cute. Always have."

The elevator jolted to a stop, reaching my level as I turned to face the reflective door. Never had I felt so completely empowered, so totally in control as my one hidden truth finally came out in the most spectacular way. It was effortlessly seamless when I turned back with a seductive wink.

I faced forward, smiling at my reflection for a second, waiting for the door to open.

Nothing.

Nick reached for the button and pressed it.

I continued to stare.

Nothing again.

The elevator door wasn't opening.

It.

Wasn't.

Opening.

Reason #7

He Makes Me Feel Safe, Even While Pushing My Buttons

Elena

"Oh, that's not good," Nick mumbled while the elevator buzzed with an annoying alarm.

I pushed him aside, my tiny elbow knocking him away as I frantically pressed the buttons.

"What did you do?" I asked loudly, partially to Nick, partially to me. I admitted he was cute—*actually cute*—my last declaration like some magical incantation that locked us in this metal shoebox. How? Why? Was I really stuck in here after confessing that?

"I didn't do anything," Nick assured calmly. "These old elevators sometimes need a little help."

"Well, you're the help, right?"

"I'm the super."

"Doesn't that involve this?"

"This is a little outside my wheelhouse." Nick laid his bags on the floor, hovering over my shoulder.

"This requires an engineer sometimes... though I doubt it's serious."

I pulled out my phone and sighed, the screen completely black, entirely dead. "You have to call someone!"

"I don't have my phone... but it's ok, there's a button here for service."

"Are they fast? Could we fall?" I turned toward him, worried.

Maybe death by elevator wouldn't be so bad, a swifter and more merciful sentence than being stuck with Nick after telling him how I felt. My antlers jingled back and forth as I switched between facing Nick and the buttons.

"Yes, they're fast. And no one is falling."

"It's New York, it's happened before."

"I won't let it happen to you," Nick's hand reached toward my waist, pressing the emergency call button. "If we fall, I'll lift you up."

"Lift me?" I squeaked.

"Yes... I'll make sure you're secure before we hit the bottom. I'll hold you in my arms and lie on my back."

"Does that work?" I froze, quickly swiping my headband off.

"Of course. It's elevator safety 101. But we're not falling," Nick laughed.

I stared up at him, horrified at how stupid I looked again. He seemed focused on the buttons as I stood frigid, concerned that I had somehow creeped him out with my comment.

Was it too much?

Would he still come fix my sink eventually?

I hated to think that my quick admission would soon become an awkward tombstone to our relationship. Before I blurted out to Nick, I imagined leaving this elevator, and allowing my confidence to do the convincing on how sexy I could be.

This whole scenario was quite literally the opposite of what Camilla suggested!

Ugh, I'm such a mess.

Nick, though?

He seemed unfazed.

In fact, he fought a smile as he locked his eyes onto mine, almost laughing at how shocked I must have appeared.

"Is this funny to you, Nicholas Stafford!" I shouted.

Nicholas?

Did I just use his full name?

He inched closer, nearly sandwiching me against the wall and intercom.

"It's a little funny," he whispered sweetly, sending me into an almost hypnotic calmness.

"*MAP communications, this is Linda, how may I help you?*" An older woman's voice came through the intercom as Nick cleared his throat.

"Hi, yes. We seem to be stuck in our elevator."

"*Residential or commercial?*" she asked. I couldn't help but pipe in.

"Residential! There's an alarm going off, and I'm trying to exit the fifth floor."

"*Do you see the button with two arrows facing the opposite directions?*"

"You mean the one I keep smashing." Nick and I took turns pecking at it.

"*Yes. Stop clicking it.*"

Nick rubbed his chin as he spoke patiently. "I'm thinking one of the emergency switches was accidentally triggered."

"*Most likely... do you see the 'Push Run' button?*"

"Yes."

"*Is it engaged?*"

"How can you tell?"

"*Before you press anything, let me get your address in case we get disconnected. I can dispatch the fire department over there in seconds.*"

Yes, god, send anyone! A firefighter, a construction worker, a deli owner, anyone at all who could free us from this thing. I leaned into Nick so the lady could hear me. "Thank you! We're down in SOHO, Prince Street, 143—"

I could barely get the numbers out, as Nick twisted a knob.

Immediately the alarm went off.

Along with the lights.

"Oh, shit," Nick whispered.

"Nicholas!"

Full name? Two times in a row?

A red emergency light slowly came on from above, barely illuminating our faces in the dimly lit elevator. Nick twisted the knob again, but the lady on the other end was gone, left only with the first three numbers of our address.

I tired not to panic as I turned to Nick with the widest eyes ever.

He grinned apologetically, lifting up the

large *Sichuan Garden* bag as an offering. "Hungry?"

"I'm not sure if I want to admit this..." Nick chuckled to himself. We sat on the dark elevator floor, slurping down noodles and sesame chicken. He passed me another crab wonton, his hand and features visible in the cast of the mellow red light above.

"Oh, come on! It can't be that bad. All Christmas movies are a little silly, anyways. So which one's your favorite?"

"It's a divisive answer, I swear."

"What? *Christmas with the Kranks?*"

Nick held out his hand as if stopping me. "Woah... don't diss the Kranks." He stabbed his chopsticks into his takeout container, dividing the assorted vegetables from the picked over meat. "Ok. Here it is. I know it's not pretty, but try not to judge... promise?"

"Promise."

It was dark, but I could tell Nick squinted in my direction. He paused, then spoke into his napkin. "It's *Home Alone... Two*."

I coughed up sweet and sour sauce, obviously judging him and not keeping my promise. "Two!"

"Hey! Don't be rude."

"I'm sorry, but that's blasphemy. One is the original, it's untouchable. Two?"

"I'm a New Yorker, what can I say? It's the same movie as the first, but in our city. It's way better."

"He's not even *home* alone in that one!"

"He is at one point... alone in a home. It gets by on technicality." Nick reached into his endless bag of Chinese food to hand me napkins and an egg roll. I took both from his hand, still laughing at how appalled he was by my response.

"Is this to shut me up?" I asked, taking a quick bite, wiping sauce off my chin.

"Trying to make amends for offending you with my movie taste... wait till you hear my thoughts on *Jingle All the Way*." Nick turned his attention back to his food, but I didn't dare look away.

It'd been over thirty minutes since the power went out, but I didn't mind any more. Sure, I was a little drunk, still semi-mortified, but Nick was being totally cool. The emergency panel was still open, the speaker still silent, but I wasn't that bothered. Here in the dark, munching on food, laughing, it almost felt romantic, *kinda* like a date.

I ignored the fantasy, the ridiculous notion that us being stuck in an elevator could ever be considered something as exciting as going out to dinner with Nick Stafford. Yet, wasn't that what we were doing?

"Thank you," I said quickly.

Nick perked up.

"Pardon?"

"Thank you for making me feel better. I know I was freaking out earlier, but you... fixed that. Guess that's what you do, though. You fix things, and not just the plumbing. I don't know what I'd do if I were alone right now."

Nick took a few more bites, then shrugged.

"I'd find you." He nodded. "Just like someone will find us. It's late, and people are either out celebrating tonight, or already in bed."

"Maybe Marty will come to our rescue," I joked, but Nick was quick to reply.

"His bowl is full of food, and he's watching *Seinfeld* right now. He won't even know I'm missing."

"So, he isn't expecting this giant sack of Chinese food?"

Nick furrowed. "It was more of a Christmas

surprise... the old boy will still get a treat once I'm back."

We both chewed a little longer, taking turns crossing our legs, making due with the space we had. Nick's long legs would spread out from time to time, his large boot resting near my thigh. I kept my legs tight together, our walls made of mirrors, giving me all the opportunity to accidentally flash Nick if I weren't careful. It was dark though, maybe I could get away with it, my panties still hidden enough that I carefully relaxed more in my posture.

"So... why were you all dressed up tonight? I know you were with your boss, but..." he didn't finish his sentence, he only arched a perfectly intrigued brow.

"There was sorta a Christmas party tonight."

"Sorta?"

"Well... a big one. But it ended up having to do with my deadline, so I was on the clock, but with cocktails, of course."

"Oh! A work party." He seemed sensitive to the subject, pausing after the word *work*. Oh, god, of course, he was thinking of this morning, of the package I so pathetically declared was for my job.

"I'm actually doing a small assignment: *Twelve Days of Sex-Mas*."

"Never heard that version of the song before," he joked.

"It's better than the song. This one will actually make you hit the *high* notes." I shamelessly plugged in one of my Instagram captions.

"Explains the package today."

"Yeah... The August Falls toy."

"And which day was that one for?"

"Second to last." I swallowed my spit, chewing more Chinese food than maybe I should've. My mouth felt entirely too dry, and Nick seemed to notice.

"Thirsty?"

"A little."

Nick reached into the paper grocery bag, moving items aside as he revealed a crystalline bottle of Havana Club Rum. He twisted it with a pop. "Looked good at the store, thought it could bring a little holly to my jolly." He sniffed it, then took a long sip, letting it sit in his mouth. He made me laugh, but the way his cheeks contoured to the bottle, his Adam's apple bobbing with a swallow, felt oddly masculine and entirely hot. He exhaled, absolutely pleased. "Interested?"

"Always." I leaned over to take the bottle. "Now this is Christmas." I took a swig, the liquor still chilled from the Manhattan wind. I shivered as the punch of alcohol hit my chest.

"You know, technically, it's not Christmas till you get a gift." Nick motioned to Camilla's package.

"Oh, no, no... that's for later."

"How so?"

"It's my next assignment."

Nick smiled. "Don't tell me, twelve drummers drumming?"

"That would be hard to rate, I'm used to only one drummer drumming, if you know what I mean." I passed the bottle back to Nick as he took another sip.

"And how does one rate the toys of *Sex-Mas?* Price? Practicality?"

"Pleasure," I burped. *Fuck.* I wiped my face, fixing my hair as I straightened my posture. "Sorry."

"No need to apologize. That was cute. Maybe even cuter than this intriguing little countdown of yours. But how is the pleasure assessed? Is it by customer reviews?"

"Not exactly..." I pinned my attention to the glittery tips of my heels, wondering if this was a good topic to discuss. Would it be so bad considering he admitted to liking *Home Alone Two?* I tried to convince myself that this was some sort of vulnerable flaw he trusted me with, that this silly preference made him not only human, but approachable. Maybe it was the fresh hit of rum, but my ridiculous reasoning made sense. "Actually, I review them... personally."

"Including August Falls?" he asked, intrigued.

"It's for *work*."

"I'll take that as a yes."

"He's very popular, you know. There's a reason he's number two on the list. Do you know who he is?"

"I'm aware of him..."

"How aware?" I jabbed inquisitively, truly curious.

"I've seen him perform... he's done scenes with some of my favorites."

"You have favorites?"

"Yes. Don't you?"

I set my takeout down on the floor, reaching for the bottle of rum. "Maybe. August Falls is probably my top pick... yours?"

Nick twisted his lips, silently biting the inside of his cheek. "I don't watch too much... but I certainly have a type."

"What's her name?" I dared him with a whisper.

"Madison Love."

I instantly knew who she was. In fact, I watched her with August Falls today. I could've sworn she was Latina, but couldn't tell for sure. My heart raced at his admission. "She's petite," I said, acting nonchalant.

"She has dark hair, and a nice olive tan. I'd prefer if her eyes were brown, though. That's what I like... amongst other things. But there is no one on film that fully captures what I'm really wanting... or who." Nick folded his hands together, probably feeling unsure if he had made the right move in telling me. "So, you like August, huh?"

"Of course, what girl doesn't?"

"How about his toy?"

I took another drink, then passed it back.

"Let's just say... he passed my test."

"Five stars?"

"Mmmmhmm..." I tried not to fidget, but the way Nick stared at me, the crimson light on his sharp features and chiseled chin burned down my arms. "I watched him today... for my assignment."

"Tell me about it," he instructed, not sternly, but confidently, as if it were natural and expected.

"I, uh... watched him with Madison Love, actually. They were in an alley, having sex behind a nightclub in the dark. Felt homemade... spontaneous even." I blushed, my face dropping as I realized what I just admitted. Did I really say that? "I'm so sorry. I know we shouldn't be talking about this."

"About what?" Nick had the most perplexing, eyebrow arching expression.

"You know... *porno.*" I mouthed the last part of my sentence, as if the word itself would summon my abuelita with her disciplinary chancla. This was so wrong.

"Porn? Really? Oh... I'm not bothered by that at all." Nick shrugged, as if it were no big deal, when in actuality my entire upbringing begged to differ.

"We don't really talk about sex where I come from. It's a 'keep it to yourself' kinda topic."

"That's like ignoring an itch that needs to be scratched."

"My mother would disagree." I flashed an awkward smile, keeping my cool. I wasn't sure if I said too much, or if I was now considered un-ladylike —like how my family would perceive it.

Nick bumped his boot against my thigh.

"I promise it's ok. You don't need to feel ashamed for something that's as natural as sex. You're safe to be yourself with me." He pointed to the metal walls around us. "This is a judgment-free zone. Besides, I know exactly what video you're talking about. It's actually really hot."

My eyes shot wide open. My mouth dropped.

"So hot!" I blurted, unapologetically.

"And the ending..."

"God, the *ending*," I emphasized, hypnotized by the outdoor creampie that dribbled all over Madison Love's ankle adorned panties.

We both laughed, relaxed in the fact that we both knew exactly what we were talking about. Nick's chuckle slowed into a sigh. He wanted to ask me something. I just knew it. He licked his chopsticks before looking me straight in the eyes.

"So... how did the toy feel going in?" he asked, his gravelly tone reaching from across the elevator.

Was I ready to reveal my dirty side? Normally I was reserved, but my current state of mind was as loose as my drunken lips. Anyways, Nick was pretty cool about sex, treating it more like a casual conversation about the weather rather than a lecture on sin.

"It felt like heaven... I stuck it on my shower wall and used it before getting clean... my laptop was on the counter, my shower curtain pulled all the way open." I wanted to laugh from my candidness, but Nick seemed so pleased with my answer. He swooped his hair back with his hand, his smile a dirty little taunt.

"How soon after I left did you do this?"

"I was on a time crunch..."

"How... soon?" he asked calmly.

"I... did it as soon as you left. I had to."

Could this be the confidence Camilla talked about? Because it sure was getting Nick's attention as he tried his hardest to keep cool, steepling his hands before cracking his knuckles.

"Hmmm. I love the way you worded that, '*I had to*'," he repeated, sitting with it, mulling over the phrase. "And, is there anything else you *have* to do right now?" He motioned to my gift. "Since we're stuck here, don't you want to see what your next assignment is?"

I picked at my nails, not sure what to do, or how exposed the next toy would make me feel. Did I really want to open this in front of him?

"What else do you have in your paper bag?" I asked curiously, acknowledging the unmentioned items still left inside from where he pulled the rum out.

"Oh, no you don't. I showed you my booze... Now don't you want to show me your gift?"

This felt like an opportunity to play it cool like Nick.

"Knowing my boss, it could be pretty salacious." I lifted the package, untying its glittery bow, pretending indifference. "But I suppose we're past that." Carefully, I ripped the candy cane paper apart, opening the box it contained. I stared inside for a second, slightly underwhelmed by what I saw.

"Well?" Nick asked. "What is it?"

"*Secrets or Steam...* a lovers card game?" I scrunched my nose. "This is supposed to beat out August Falls?"

I read the back out loud, wrapping my mind around what could possibly be better than having a porn star inside me.

"*Secrets or Steam: the hottest new sex card game where couples complete a series of truths or dares while avoiding physical contact. The key is to not touch your opponent, no matter how tempting it may get. If a player refuses to answer a truth or enact a dare, they must remove an article of clothing that their opponent selects. Whoever touches their opponent first loses.*"

"Interesting." Nick narrowed his eyes onto the gift.

"I'm not sure if this is the right game..." I said, garnering his attention.

"Let's decide for ourselves. I'm ready to play."

Reason #9
His Reindeer Games Are X-Rated
Elena

Nick carefully split the cards, steepled them, then shuffled them downwards. The pile in his hand fluttered into a perfectly stacked tower, which he divided into three distinct rows.

"You nervous at all?" I thumbed the open bottle of rum. "All things considered... this is a game meant for couples."

"It's meant for two adults. And to answer your question, no, I'm not nervous... per se. There's a fine line between nervousness and excitement." Nick swiped at his forehead with the back of his hand. It was warm in here, and the glow of his face was soft and dewy. "I might be somewhere in between, actually."

"Between nervous and excited?" I leaned against the mirrored wall. "What would you call it?"

"Adventurous?" Nick settled on an answer. "I

don't know if this will be good or bad. It's risky... but that's how anything is ever discovered. It's pulling the curtain back on something mysterious and taking a chance on the unknown. And who doesn't like that?"

If mystery was what Nick liked, then I was a little short of being anything but. Nearly an hour ago I admitted I thought he was cute. Now? We sat on the floor, sorting cards to a sex game I was in charge of rating. It was surreal, something between a dream and a nightmare, the horror of being stuck in a dark elevator, with the fantasy of being close to Nick. Maybe like him, I was both nervous and excited, wondering how far we'd go, or if I'd accidentally ruin the good time we were having. How long could this last until I embarrassed myself again?

"Well, there's no pressure with this. It's just a game," I shrugged.

Nick lowered his voice, his presence calming. "It'll be fun. Games are supposed to be fun."

"Fun is good. I like fun," I rambled, stealing his sentiment.

"*Fun*... were those little antlers you wore earlier," he teased, "and like you said, no pressure. At any point you want to stop, you tell me... I have plenty of fortune cookies that we can crack open and read out loud for kicks."

I fidgeted, our back and forth a subtle excuse to defuse the tension the cards provoked. Each pile was a different intensity, color, and steam level for the dares and questions to come. "First base, second base, third?" I read the cards out loud. "Where's the home run?"

"Guessing that comes after one of the opponents loses." Nick motioned his palm in my direction, revealing the stacks that were ready to be played. "Ladies first."

I sat up straight. Obviously, I wanted to start simple, so I reached for a *first base* card, my hand on the verge of shaking.

Nick smirked.

I flipped over a *secret* card and began to giggle. "Oh, god."

"Is it ridiculous?"

"No. Just a little silly. Ok... here we go. Pick one, '*Whipped Cream or Candle Wax?*'" I playfully fanned the card towards my cheek, pursing my candy-apple red lips.

Nick brushed the tips of his knuckles along his jaw, contemplating. "Whipped cream."

"Why?"

"Do I need to explain?" he laughed.

"Yeah, why not?" I passed back the bottle of rum.

"Cream... because it's sweet... it's lickable. You

can place it on someone, or on each other, but removing it is the best part."

"And where would you put it?" I asked boldly, consciously avoiding biting my lip.

"I'd put some above your navel... I'd lick it all the way up." He said, challenging me with a stare. Did he say *your* navel, as in, mine? I swallowed, trying not to choke.

"You'd do that to me?"

"Isn't that how we're supposed to answer?"

"Oh, I don't know... that makes sense."

"Should I apologize?" Nick asked, not panicked, not worried, but inquisitive, almost daring me to say yes, as if doing so would have consequences. I crossed my legs again.

"No need."

"Then I'll go next." Nick reached for a *first base* card, which he seemed to immediately appreciate.

"I'm already dreading it."

"No, no. It's a good one. You can tell a lot about a person by how they answer this, and you only have two choices, no context... '*Top or Bottom*'?"

Are you kidding me?

A highlight reel of sex positions sputtered wildly in my imagination.

Heavy panting, grunting, screaming.

I'd take it any way I could get it with Nick, my

legs above my head, or my thighs hugging his hips—hips I rocked over, fucking him into a ball-draining, shaft-glistening climax.

I cleared my throat, ending the millisecond flash of passion with a quick nonchalant answer.

"If I were with you... I'd ride on top." I reached for a card to move on, but Nick's hand hovered over the stack. I stopped short of touching him.

"Why top?"

I slowly removed my hand, hesitating. "Just... better control. I guess."

"Over me?"

"Over... how I'm entered." I avoided his face, scanning his shoulders down to his strong hands. "You're a big guy. I'm not sure if I could take all of you. On top I can slip down easier."

I'm pretty sure my insides were sweating at this point!

Nick chewed the corner of his lip. "You a tight girl, Elena?"

God, his deep voice was enough to cause my bad decisions to play out. "Maybe." I maintained a poker face. "I mean... with the right person I can get wet easily, but it takes a while to adjust."

"And by adjust you mean, stretch?"

The way he enunciated the word *stretch* was as sharp as it was precise. I bit my tongue to keep from laughing, not that it was funny, but completely surreal.

"Yes. That way I can move my hips. Bounce. Rub." I paused, then spoke quickly. "If I can fit you completely inside, then I can grind myself on your body. And that's something I like." I said matter of fact. The alcohol was clearly bringing out my honesty, "Or, on *anyone's* body for that matter."

Nick's nonresponse was just as much of a response than anything, punctuated with that sexy little nod of his. I wanted him on the receiving end of embarrassment, taking my chance and immediately reaching for a second base card. I expected the look of fear on his face, but his narrow focus said otherwise.

"Nick," I began confidently. "'*Fuck me, marry me, or date me?*'"

"Seriously?"

"Blame it on the cards." I flicked it in his direction.

"And if I don't answer that?"

"Then... you remove a piece of your clothing... one of *my* choosing." I pointed in his direction, hoping he'd answer, but also secretly hoping he wouldn't.

He dragged his hands down his face,

contemplative, his index finger tapping the dip below his nose.

"I'll skip that one."

"Really?"

"Yes. I won't answer that."

"Bit of a prude?"

"Not in the least," he chuckled. "I'm just more curious as to what piece of clothing you'd want me to remove..."

Conservatively speaking, I had a lot to choose from. Jacket or boots were an obvious choice, but that'd make me into the very same *prude* I accused him of. A part of me wanted him to regret his choice, and a part of me wanted to enjoy something new I hadn't seen of him before.

"Your sweater." I demanded, "Take it off."

Nick didn't react; in fact, he followed my eyes, studying my reaction as he removed his jacket first, peeling it off his shoulders, tossing it towards the corner behind me. "You sure you want my sweater?"

"Off, big guy," I instructed once more.

Nick reached down to the hem of his soft cotton sweater, his knuckles molded and tight, effortlessly lifting it up. First were the lean cuts of his abs, a sight I'd seen before while he laid under my sink: firm and ripped with trimmed black hair that rose towards his navel, a navel framed with hard, olive abs that stretched to his side. His hair was wavy and brown, lighter than the patch that laid over his well-worked chest.

"That wasn't so hard... now was it?" I choked, his woodsy scent wafted from my lap as he tossed his sweater towards me. I fisted it in my hands.

Nick reached for another card. "I don't think you're ready for a second base card, so I'll go for first."

"Oh, stop. I'm ready. These aren't even that bad."

"No?" he questioned, lifting a first base card. "Ok, then '*Describe Your Panties to Me*'."

I scrunched my nose, almost bored by the laughable question asked by a shirtless Nick. I could be edgy; I could be like him. "No," I answered. "Pick a clothing item for me to remove. I'll do that instead."

Without hesitation, Nick ordered me immediately, "I want you to remove your panties for me."

I froze.

Describing them was so boring, but now, I was supposed to take them off? Quickly, I ran through my mind, trying to recall what I wore and if they were any good. Were they my comfortable, loose, cotton panties, or something Camilla would approve of? I tried not to hesitate, overwhelmed by how small the elevator suddenly felt.

I caught a glimpse of the security camera in the corner, nodding toward it, "Do you think anyone can see us?"

Nick looked over his shoulder. "That camera? Nah, that's impossible."

"Why? Because it's too dark in here?"

"Because, it hasn't been working since Mrs. Caporali hit it with a hammer. She does that with a lot of things, actually."

Duh.

"Right. Okay. Turn around."

"Did you turn around when I took off my sweater? I recall you looking quite intently… so much so I think you enjoyed it, Miss Elena Ortiz," he said with authority, a cadence that weakened my knees as I stood up.

"Then try not to drool," I sneered, watching the amusement on his face as I carefully reached beneath my skirt, momentarily lifting it, pinching my thighs as if that would stop my skin from showing.

Nick's attention shifted between my legs and waist, stitching his focus to the hint of my panties that appeared for a moment.

I sighed with relief when I felt my frilly, red lace thong. The graze of my own touch made me so aware of my body, realizing now as I stood how my clit thrummed with a pulse. I tried not to react, but I was turned on, my panties pathetically damp with a wetness I hadn't even realized had been seeping out. Was it the game? Was it Nick? Everything felt piled on as I shimmed my hips.

My panties fell to my heels, their elastic band loose around my ankles as I lifted them free.

"Toss them to me," Nick instructed, playing a dangerous game.

"Absolutely not!" I squeaked, challenged by his tempting, deep voice.

"You a prude?"

"As if!" I defended, unknowingly morphing into Cher Horowitz.

"You sure about that?"

"Yes. I'm *totally* on the naughty list." I shrugged, feeling a little silly, but I didn't care because my drunkenness mellowed out into a calming buzz. And although I was sobering up, I confidently tossed them over.

Nick snatched them in the air, its band laced on his thumb, the entirety of its fabric swallowed by his hand. He had the strength to rip them off my body had I still had them on, his forearms firm and corded. God, Camilla was right, he did look like Henry Cavill.

"Red. My favorite color," he mused.

I wondered if he felt my wetness, his attention

diverted to where his finger traced the fabric's inner layer before shoving them in his pocket.

"And your underwear?" I asked.

"Excuse me?"

"Describe them to me. Boxers or briefs?" I sat back down, carefully crossing my legs.

"You want me to answer a steamy question for free?"

"Sure! Naughty girls can't just get coal. Tell me."

Nick pondered for a second, then settled his eyes to the ground. "Honestly. None. I don't wear them often, and I certainly don't wear them to bed."

Really?

He wore nothing?

Nick nude and tangled in the cool sheets of a large bed flashed in my head, his back puckered, his ass peeking and toned from the loose covering of Egyptian cotton. I supposed it was believable, having seen his pants in the past dipping below his pelvis, his natural V-shape visible without the confinement of the Calvin Klein underwear I imagined he'd wear.

I eyed him suspiciously, reaching for a second base card. "*Would you ever want to watch me have sex with someone else?*" I asked.

"Someone else?" He seemed simultaneously intrigued and conflicted. "Another man?"

"Could be a woman."

"That'd be better. But I wouldn't care to see it at all."

"Really?"

"Not that I wouldn't want to see what's under that skirt... or that top... to see you bare, without another person's hands or body on it, man or woman. In fact, I can't imagine how I'd react if I ever saw that... upset? Jealous?"

I almost missed his words as my heart pounded in my ears. I wanted to say something but couldn't, still stuck on the idea that Nick Stafford could ever be jealous of anyone else touching me. "What?" I asked, as he shuffled all the cards together; bases one, two and three into one unanimous pile.

"Pick another card. Ask me. Dare me. Do it again," he asserted.

Hesitantly, I lifted another mild first base question. My voice swayed, unaware of how adrenaline took hold of my tone. "*'What's the biggest lie you've ever told to get close to someone?'*" I folded the card to my chest.

"I've told a lot. They're innocent, but still lies."

"And the biggest of them all?"

"One that I'm not ready to share yet. It may be more embarrassing than you think."

"I know all too well about being embarrassed." I admitted, our eyes locked in a gaze.

"You think you've embarrassed yourself in front of me?"

"All the time. It seems to be what I do best. Haven't you noticed?"

Nick clenched his teeth, disappointed. "Whatever you think is embarrassing, is actually endearing..."

"By whom?"

"Guess," he dared me.

I grew silent, unable to say what I thought he was implying, so I avoided answering him. "You didn't answer my question. Now you have to remove a piece of your clothing."

"And what would you want?"

"Your belt," I settled.

Nick reached for his buckle, threading his thumb between the brass, meticulously undoing it. It clinked in his hand, the leather snapping loose as he yanked it through the loops of his fitted chinos. His abs expanded, his pants less constricting, comfortably snug with the tiniest gap of skin that hinted towards his crotch.

"Let's both pull cards. One last time, that is... if you're up for the challenge..." He tapped his finger on the third base card sitting at the top of the deck. Its red, glossy finish taunted me with the risk of being asked the craziest question, or the dirtiest dare.

"You take the top. And I'll take the next one," I instructed, allowing Nick to remove the third base card, and for me to take a first base card below. "You go first," I whispered.

Nick read his card, then asked, "Are you sure you're a naughty-list girl?"

"Mmhmm," I nodded.

"How naughty?"

"Naughty enough to tell you how I fucked myself in the shower. Isn't that naughty enough?"

"Close. But this card wants more. Are you brave enough for it?"

I twisted a loose curl that fell to the side of my face, curious as to what the card said. I wanted to be committed, I wanted to take a risk, just like Camilla said. Confidence was sexy, and I was done feeling like I was second to anyone else. "I'll do it for you," I whispered.

"Elena... *'Show me how you masturbate,'*" Nick ordered, his voice carrying up from his chest; heated and deep.

Masturbate?

I could never. Not with how I was raised. Not with the shame of everything it entailed. But something inside me snapped. A decision beyond my compression.

My heart pounded so fast it tingled the tips of my

fingers. "Will you show me, too?" I asked nervously, not wanting to back out, but letting my heart take control.

"If you want me to, I will... but let's start slow." Nick cocked his head as we both gradually stood up. I felt sheepish and small next to him, his height towering across from mine. "I can shut my eyes if you'd like."

"Could you," I replied. "Just at first? Until I'm ready?"

"That's fine." Nick ran his hand across his torso, grazing his abs, dropping past his navel. "I'll meet you wherever you want to go with this, as long as your eyes are on me." He shut his eyes, his face furrowed with a deep concentrated breath. "Just place your hand where you like it, and I'll do the same."

I lifted my skirt as Nick unbuttoned his pants, his zipper unraveling with its enticing metallic lure. He reached further down, the impression of his cock molded against his pants as he fisted the base of his erection. I nearly lost my breath at how big he was, how aroused he became, swollen just like my clit.

Carefully, I tested how sensitive I'd become, little jolts of warm electricity tingled from the tip of my index finger right onto the spot I rubbed, my pussy slippery but tight.

"You there, yet?" he asked, eyes still closed.

"Yes." My breathing hitched from how he squeezed his cock. He stroked himself just once, his pants too tight for anything but a slow, smooth jerk.

"Elena, are you touching yourself?"

"Yes. I'm just... so sensitive right now." I cautiously circled my clit, my knees buckling in and out with the bundled nerves that needled through my thighs. Nervousness still took hold of my every move, my body slowly warming up to the idea of being watched.

Nick's pants dropped further towards his pelvis, revealing a tan line that met the neat patch of dark pubic hair and flat muscle. "Are you watching me stroke myself?"

"Yes. It looks tight against your thigh... I think it's sexy." I shuddered, dipping my finger inside my slit, finding the courage to thrust it inside me, freeing my wetness. "Can you hear how wet I am?"

Nick stroked harder, his head leaning against the elevator wall, eyes squeezed shut. "You still embarrassed to do this?"

"No," I answered immediately, so quickly that I almost giggled. It was liberating actually, and I rubbed myself harder.

"Does it make you shy that I can hear your wet little cunt?" he gritted, and it turned me on.

"I want you to hear." A moan escaped me, as I unzipped the side of my skirt. "You can look now." I said hesitantly, ready for his needy eyes to be on me, convincing myself that it was ok since he knew I fucked myself for work, that I watched porn and played with my holes.

Nick's mouth parted with a breath, his eyes clear and vivid as he opened them, seemingly aching by the sight of me, by the fact that he wasn't able to touch me.

"Jesus, Elena. You're so fucking beautiful." The mounds of his shoulders tightened as his pants fell past his ass, his cock springing loose.

"Fuck," I ran my fingers past my clit, bobbing in and out of my pussy, spreading myself open so he could jerk off to it. At first all I could see was Nick, his erection stiff in his hands, far larger than the grip he used to wrap around the entirety of his dick. He licked up his palm, stroking the tip of his cock into his fist.

"Is that how you do it? You finger yourself?"

I pumped faster, shutting my eyes, then opening them again, controlling my breath. I showed off my stomach, taking hold of my shirt, lifting it up for Nick, for his insatiable expression, for him to see the soft, flat spot below my breast as I leaned against the wall. "I always finger myself. Always. I love the way it feels."

"Tell me," he instructed.

I tried not to lean forward, fighting the beginning tingles of an orgasm as Nick's tempting cock glistened with spit, his balls waiting to be drained. Fuck, why did that turn me on so damn much? Was this really happening? It felt like a dream, and the longer we played, the more real it became.

"I like the pressure of being entered. Of feeling open, and if I had it with me, I'd fuck myself with my toy."

"You'd do that... for me?"

"Just for you," I swallowed. "But fuck, Nick, don't go too fast, it makes me want to go fast too, and I'm not ready for this to be over."

"Then do it with me," he squeezed tighter, rocking his hips into his hand. I bit into the bottom of my shirt, unintentionally lifting it past my bra, its black lace taut on my tits, my nipples escaping as I arched my back and heaved my chest.

"Just... if you fucking come. Could you come on me?" I whimpered.

"You'd want that, naughty-list girl?" he asked eagerly.

"All over my stomach." My first base card fell out

of my hand, my head wild and spinning as it caught Nick's attention.

I froze as he pulled his pants up, making his way toward me. I almost screamed when he nearly pinned me against the wall.

"Nick!" I yelped as he moved far closer than he'd ever been before. The heat of his cock sat bent in his hand, almost grazing my stomach as I palmed my pussy. I didn't move an inch, not wanting to lose the game.

He looked down at my card on the floor.

"Read it for me," he breathed me in. "Ask me what the card says, because I'm fucking dying to tell you."

I peeked over at it, the innocent question so simple and sweet compared to how hot we just got.

"*'What outfit do I look the sexiest in?'*" I muttered near his lips.

"Would you believe me if I told you this: a pink robe, a towel in your hair, green cream on your face... you. You from this morning. You from last week with the red sweater and gold hoop earrings. You from the summer, with your white tank top and your small— oh so fucking tight—denim shorts. It's you, it's your curly hair, your red lips, and brown eyes... eyes that are more caramel than cinnamon, a color that I have carefully and constantly contemplated about."

"Nick?" I wanted to fall back, but was already against the elevator wall: blushing, hot with a sticky sweat that took over my entire body.

"Do you really think I'm cute?" he asked.

My eyes watered. Sad? Excited? Overwhelmed?

"Yes. I do," I said timidly.

"And what if I told you I felt the same? What if I told you that the biggest lie I ever said to get to someone was with you? That I could've fixed your sink by now, but have delayed it, just so that I could see you more, or that all this food I got tonight wasn't just for me, but for us. What if I told you that in that paper bag behind us were all the ingredients for coquito, that I wanted to make you feel like you were home again? Everything I do is secretly for you because I want you, and even though I know it's dangerous to get involved, I'll do it, because I'd rather lose you now, than live another second not telling you how I feel." He gravitated closer, his breath sweet like rum and mint.

"You mean that, Nick? You did all this for me?" I tried not to cry, resisting the urge to leap up and kiss him.

"Just for you, Elena. I want to do everything for you. I wanted to spend tonight with you, which is a much better holiday than anything I could've imagined... and that's why we're still stuck here."

"What do you mean?" I asked.

"It means... if I told you I could've really fixed this elevator by now, would you be mad at me?"

His confession settled into my chest, a bombshell truth that caused my eyes to water. It was crazy, it was wild, but most of all, it was something that felt so endearing, only because it was Nick—my Nick—a man who never once judged me like I judged myself.

"I could never be mad at you," I said.

Nick leaned in, his forehead settling onto mine. His breath, his touch, his heat, turned me on and made me throb. "You lost the game," I said, hopelessly delighted that he was the first to make contact.

"Did I?" he smiled. "Maybe I actually just won?"

"Maybe..."

Nick said nothing.

He gritted and leaned in further, my body shaking from the touch of his bristled, five o'clock shadow, as my palms caught on fire, turning our seconds into minutes, our minutes into hours, and those hours into an infinite pool of time and stars that exploded behind my eyes.

His lips pressed against mine.

Nick's!

My stomach instantly fluttered, my body a shell of bull riding heartbeats that bucked wildly as Nick moaned my name, his kiss sweeter than the sweetest rum from Puerto Rico.

And as I melted against the elevator wall, I rubbed my clit faster, harder, greedy to kiss him back, not caring if it felt desperate, because that's how I felt, and I was grateful for how honest it made me feel.

He was a god, he was an angel, mischievous yet sweet. He was Nick-fucking-Stafford.

"Do you want me to open the elevator?" He asked sweetly, his cock slipping free and onto my stomach.

"Don't," I warned, his fingers interlacing with mine. "Not until we're done."

Reason #10

HE KNOWS ME INSIDE AND OUT

Nick

Of all the wrong things to do, of all the warning signs I learned from my sister and her divorce—how not to be involved with those you work around, live around—this was the test I knew I'd fail. It was wrong to lie to Elena, and it was wrong to touch her, but fuck if I couldn't resist the urge to graze my finger—hell, my pinky—across the smooth, tanned spot right above her bellybutton.

"I should be gentle, but it's so goddamn hard not to devour you right now." I seethed into her curls, her arms wrapped around my shoulders. "I feel like I've waited for so long, and the longer it's been, the hungrier I've gotten." Slowly my pants fell loose as I kicked off my boots, standing tall against Elena's soft skin, her chin raised to my chest as I brushed my nose down her head and onto her cheek.

"Just kiss me. Lift me and let me taste your lips.

I've wanted to kiss you for so long," she whined sweetly. "Savor it. Savor me."

"Every inch." I claimed her, her ass mantled onto my palms as I pushed my weight against her and the elevator wall, wedging her near the railing for support. "You're so hot, Elena... so, so hot. I can feel it between your legs." I kissed those pouty red lips that had always belonged to me, stifling my need to fuck her hard, from thrusting the entirety of my erection right into her little slit. Savoring wasn't just what she wanted, it's what she *needed*—my complete appreciation of the only moment I ever dreamed of.

"You can really feel me?" she shuddered, surprised.

"Of course." I tried not to answer weakly, her needy clit puffy and wet, grinding with the sway of her hips over the head of my cock, covering me with her sweet feminine scent that drove me feral. I kissed her again, licking her lips, sucking them, memorizing her scent for later, her neck and hair sweet like jasmine and strawberries.

"I like that," she moaned. "Your scruff on me, it's rough, but nice."

"Do you like it here?" I kissed behind her ear, removing her shirt, the width of my hand cupping her bra to the top of her breasts, the same breasts whose cleavage I saw tucked into her robe this morning, the cotton, pink covering that I wanted to shred apart. But now I had her, her little black bra transparent in the cup of my hands, frilled and laced with just enough covering to mask what I wanted beneath.

"Yes... there." She swallowed as I shoved her bra down, her nipples hard and sweet, tanned like butterscotch candies to my tongue that flicked and sucked them.

"And here?" My jaw clenched with restraint, brushed against her sides, her breathing shallow as I made my way down, hoisting her legs over my shoulders while bowing on my knees. "Just a taste, baby girl," I muttered, a nickname I never called her before, but came out so naturally and easily that I didn't even skip a beat. I forced Elena up against the wall, standing, gripping her hips to lick the taste out from her cunt.

"God," she begged, gripping my hair, burning my scalp with a tight squeeze that I craved. I moaned against her slit, the soft spot that my cock twitched for, stretching her open with my tongue as I fucked her with my mouth.

"I've thought of this, I've thought of you, in every position, in every scenario." My stubble bristled against her thigh as she rode herself from my tongue to the tip of my nose. I sucked her clit into my mouth, letting it loose with a loud wet pop. "And for as much as I've thought of it, I never knew where to begin... but between your legs feels so goddamn perfect. Holding you—your hips, your waist." I took hold of her sides, festering in something so biological, so mechanical and ancient. She felt built to be bred, and my body craved to be unleashed in her, to flood her full. "You make me ache."

"You just need a release. We both do," she said.

"Fuck," I groaned. "I don't have protection... I brought nothing."

"No, no... it's ok. I'm tested and clear, plus I'm on the pill." She looked down at me, hope in her eyes, "Are you—"

"I'm tested, too. I'm good." I assured, more relaxed as I kissed her torso, sliding her back down toward my hips. "Just tell me if it's too much," I whispered, Elena's eyes wincing before growing large. Her mouth parted, opening the same moment her folds wrapped around the tip of my cock, her heat meeting the most sensitive part of my body as I rested my head against hers.

"Slowly," she bated, "I like when it's slow."

"Then, I'll go as slow as I can." I pulled her off the wall, holding myself inside Elena as I lowered to my knees again. My calves tightened in the reflection, our bodies like a jigsaw of muscle and softness pressed against each other. She was so small compared to my hands, her gorgeous breasts rubbing down my chest as she sat further onto my cock, swallowing it.

"Fuck, Nick." She hugged me, shutting her eyes as she wedged further down, her ass meeting my thighs, the base of my erection submerged entirely into her body.

"That's it, baby, you're doing so good." I bit into her shoulder, praising how tight she clenched herself around me, how the beat of her heart hugged my arousal.

"Let me just rock myself against you—ride you. Can I?" she asked innocently, her hands framing my cheeks, kissing me. She smiled, the same smile that turned her dark eyes into adorable crescent moons, causing my heart to thrum, and my muscles to melt into her giving body.

"I'll have you any way you want me. *Any* way. Just stay with me, just let me be in you and feel you... the deepest part of you."

Elena slipped up and down my cock, slowly adjusting, giving me the freedom to join, to pump my hips in between, to fuck her like a machine made for her pleasure.

She reached for the rum and laughed, taking a sip, letting some of it spill out of her mouth and onto her chest before kissing me. "Shit, you're so fucking big for me."

I stole the bottle from her hand, pushing myself further inside her as she screamed with joy.

"Am I? Fuck me like you would your toy." I took a swig for myself, using my hand to caress her cheeks, to position her head. She moaned, her mouth open as I spit rum right onto her tongue, her tits wet with liquor, reflecting the sweat that soaked our bodies.

"My best fucking toy yet." She kissed me as I swung her around, lying her back on the soft wool of my oversized topcoat. Her curls sprawled out into a perfect halo of hair as she giggled. "No way, you're in that deep," she gasped, her thighs clamped onto my waist as she grunted, "Oh, god. Oh... god! Fuck yes."

"Give me everything," I begged, thrusting faster, her slippery cunt leaking onto my pelvis. She took me well, my perfect neighbor with the perfect pussy, massaging me to climax. "I won't fucking come until you do, not until I feel that orgasm dripping on my balls." I fucked her harder, feeling even more sensitive, ready to pop.

"You want all of me? Then you can have me," she warned, giving me the most sinful of ideas. "I won't tell you no, Nick, not with any part of my body."

Reason #77
He Takes My
Breath Away
Elena

"I hope you don't regret saying that." Nick pulled out, every inch of his erection more telling than the last, leaving me feeling so open and empty as he left my body. I was so fucking wet for his size, my blush burning against his palm as he thumbed my lips, smearing its red color onto my cheek. "I want to fill every piece of you, to have every one of your little holes shaped for me. Would you like that, Elena? To be fucked everywhere all at once?" He sat up on his knees, raking my hair until fisting it tight.

"You reading my mind, Nick Stafford?" I got on all fours, propping my ass up, facing him like an obedient dog ready to bow. "You fuck me like that, and I'll put you on the list as the best sex toy of the season." I kissed his thigh, running my tongue up the cut of his pelvis to his shaft. He throbbed for me, his cock hiccupping as my lips brushed over him.

"I'm not reading your mind, gorgeous, I just think we've always been in sync, but too afraid to admit it. Hell, I like you, and I want to be yours just as much as I want you to be mine."

I couldn't believe where I was and what I was doing, admiring the exhausted muscles of my building's super—my dream guy. He was so wet and sweaty, his scent more man than clean cologne, filling my chest with an unfamiliar warmth that somehow found its way into my stomach. Butterflies erupted from every inch of my body as I leaned my head onto his torso, hearing his heart pound magnificently through his body. That pound, that erratic beat was for me—all me—and my command was just as powerful over his body as his was for mine.

"Let me suck you, babe," I said, testing the nickname for myself, enamored by the glee on his face, and the surprise in his eyes.

"Mmmm, babe." He gripped my hair tighter. I grunted. "Babe, babe, babe. I like how that sounds. Say it again, but louder."

I kissed the tip of his cock, licking the surprisingly sweet cum that had already begun to bead out of him. Did he get any of it inside of me while we were fucking? A piece of him, his orgasm or the hint of it ever being in my body made me come apart. Maybe I wanted him spilled inside of me entirely, maybe I was greedy for it. Suddenly I wanted him to come so badly. "Stick that big dick in my mouth, *babe*, and I swear I'll suck it fucking dry."

"You tease," he shuddered, exhaling loudly as I took him into my mouth. He was too big, quickly reaching the back of my throat as I clenched onto his topcoat beneath me, fighting the urge not to gag. I didn't mind it though, and in fact I preferred it; hot tears formed at the corner of my eyes, as spit bubbled over his balls. The way his thighs tightened as I drooled over him and onto the floor was so exciting, his ass puckered in the reflection behind him, firm and round like an athlete. "Wait! Shit, not yet. I'm too close, Elena." Nick pulled out, luring a wild string of spit from my mouth as he pinched the tip of his erection, fighting his orgasm. His balls tightened and dropped, resisting the spasm I provoked.

"Almost had you," I gasped, wiping my mouth.

"Like I said, I don't come till you do. I'll do anything to get on that little list of yours. I'll make sure you know what number one really feels like, and it won't be from some vibrator or card game."

I couldn't believe how fast I got to my feet as Nick yanked me into the air, my tits pressed against the cool elevator wall. He handled my hips roughly, effortlessly, positioning me against his groin as I held onto the railing for support.

"I'm learning something new about you, Miss Elena Ortiz. I always knew you were a giver, but you're far too giving not to be taken care of first. Can't you see I want to spoil you? That I want to make you feel consumed in the best sense?" He smacked my ass, his question reaching the peach fuzz around my ear, sending shivers all over my body. My nipples hardened from how his cock slipped between my lips, taking advantage of how unabashedly wet I was. "You trust me?" The clink of his belt lifted from the floor. He snapped it.

I practically drooled my arousal onto the crown of his apple-hard cock, grinding back against his tip. "I do."

"And if you want me to stop, you tell me. This is for you, this is for your mind and pussy." Nick carefully wrapped the belt around my neck, taking special precaution to move slowly and carefully. He laced the black leather through the brass buckle, looping it loosely. "Say, 'tighter, baby,'" he instructed, notching the belt further towards my throat.

"Tighter, baby..." I echoed. He twisted the belt around his fist, turning it into a leash. "Tighter... tighter... tighter," I repeated, relishing in the surprising pressure it produced. "Ti—" I stopped, and he loosened it by a hair.

"Right there," he whispered, finding the perfect

spot for me to still breathe and speak, but also, for my head to feel fuzzy and light. "Has anyone taken you from behind before? This fucking peach of yours?" he asked. "God knows I fucking want it, how I've worshiped it anytime you've walked away... how I've stroked myself to the thought of it."

My breath fogged the mirror in front of my face, "Did I really make you come, just because of my ass?"

"Every time I'm around you I get so turned on... I always need a cold shower afterwards, but it hardly helps, it only delays the inevitable... me beating off in the shower, sputtering my mess onto the wall, wishing it was you that I'd spill inside of instead."

I felt something warm, something round and hard pushed between me, brushing my asshole. It was such a sensitive spot, such a unique button of pleasure that he merely pressed into, causing me to expand and accept him, to pop his perfect fucking head right into my hole.

"Nick..." I moaned with what little air I could, "Christ, that's it. Right there!" I encouraged, backing up slowly, his cock so soaked with my own spit, that no friction or pain was hardly felt. "I can take it all. I ca—" I paused, my pussy brushing against his balls.

"Every hole, baby girl." He kissed my neck, tightening the belt harder as he reached around, lifting me to my toes. His fingers were knuckles deep into my cunt, curling, finding the delicate mound of nerves before he pressed up on it.

"Shit, I feel so tight," I whimpered, weak by how his hips rocked into my ass, his fingers milking my pussy wet. Nick grunted, his face twisted in pleasure, the leather strap of the belt clutched into the chomp of his pearly white teeth.

"You like it in the ass? Fucking you from behind while fingering you like my little puppet?" he gritted.

My ass bounced into him, his thrusts clapping against me with a raw, hard fuck that made me want to scream.

"Harder, Nick. Fuck me harder." I rubbed my clit, forcing his fingers further as I began to quiver. Here I was, bent over, my lipstick smeared, and my tits pressed painfully hard against the wall, chasing an orgasm that felt too big to ever be expressed. I needed to scream, but Nick tightened the belt, stretching my ass with his fat dick as he fucked me harder than any man or toy ever had before.

"Is anyone in there?"

Fuck.

A woman's voice echoed from the floor above as she knocked on the large steel elevator doors.

I couldn't believe it. I'd recognize that horse Italian accent from anywhere. It was Mrs. Caporali, my neighbor, calling down to us. I wasn't sure why she was on the sixth floor.

"I think she's waiting for me." Nick smiled into my cheek, kissing it. "She's trying to set me up with one of her granddaughters tonight. I'm guessing she went to my apartment for an impromptu date."

I tried not to laugh, fully aware of Mrs. Caporali's reputation as a matchmaker.

"She can be pretty adamant. I don't think she's going to leave."

"Well neither am I. We're not going anywhere till you finish good and strong. It's what you deserve."

"But—" I hesitated, giddy. Nick massaged the back of my neck, the leather belt soft against my nape.

"Shhh... I'm your bull, baby, and I'll fuck you as such." Nick covered my mouth, squeezing it shut, his forearms wrapped in corded veins that muffled my groans. "But you gotta be quiet for me... I can't have my sweet Elena getting caught taking it so roughly."

I was so close, biting into his arm, my knees shaking as he entered my ass again, pulling out just enough to remind me how big he felt at my entrance.

"I can't hold on," I whined, finally losing control.

"Bite my fucking arm, baby, scream into it." Nick protected us from being caught, allowing me to cry into his arm as he railed me against the wall. My air grew tighter and tighter, causing stars to build in my head, and my vision to go bright. I was exploding and fading all at once, disappearing into the warmest puddle of nerves that turned my face numb. And as I thought I was about to lose sight of everything, Nick stripped the belt from my neck, releasing all the blood up to my cheeks and head, then back to my clit.

"Fuck!" I thought I was peeing for a second, ignoring how Mrs. Caporali knocked above us again, asking a question I couldn't even pay attention to. I didn't care if she heard, or if she knew who was in here, because I was coming harder than I ever knew possible.

"Baby, I'm going to... oh, shit—" Nick exhaled loudly, his toes curling beneath me as I heard hot wet drops of cum fall out of my ass.

"Come in me, come in me," I begged as Nick leaned onto my back, squeezing my breasts, draining everything he had into my ass, hot semen seeping over the entirety of my insides. He hugged me tighter than the belt, tighter than how his fingers felt inside me.

"Let me keep you... let me have you." Nick panted, kissing my upper back and neck, his sweat dripping onto my shoulders. His erection fell out of me, his orgasm spilling over my thigh and onto my heels. So much of him poured out from how hard he gave it to me. "God, Elena... I've waited for you for so long."

"And I've waited for you... ever since I first saw you. It's been the longest year, but the best one too... at least... now it is." I leaned the back of my head against his hard chest, savoring each kiss he gave, each needy touch he delivered, his hand clawing at my stomach for an embrace. I didn't think he'd ever let me go, and honestly, it made me want to cry with joy.

"Whoever is in there, don't worry! I'm getting help!" Mrs. Caporali called from above, her feet shuffling away. I tried not to laugh, unsure of how much she heard, or what would even happen if the door were to suddenly open. Nick and I were completely nude, and in no desire to hurry. I wasn't sure if either of us cared to be caught, taking our time to kiss, to face each other, to snuggle.

"I give us about twenty minutes until the fire department shows up... but I'll have us out in no time."

"In no time? Forget *Twelve Days of Sex-Mas,* I'm ready to write *Twelve Reasons Nick Stafford is the Perfect Christmas Gift Ever!* I'm not sure I'm ready to leave, yet."

Nick smiled. "Well, I can't have you sleeping on

the floor here... and if you think for a second I'm letting you go home alone tonight, you're crazy."

"And where are you stealing me away to, Superintendent Stafford?" I joked, tracing a patch of his chest hair with the tip of my finger.

Nick thought for a second, grinning with the most handsome dimple on his cheek. "Hmm... well, if I'm stealing you, then I'm keeping you at my place."

"You stealing me or selling me on a new apartment?"

"Convincing you..." He kissed me again, affirming my answer that was already written on my face. "One bed, one home... no leaky faucets, no more lost mail."

Reason #12
HE'S A SMART COOKIE
(ONE YEAR LATER)
Elena

"Think of it like a festival, but indoors." I fluffed up a row of bright red *pascua* flowers, keeping them away from Marty. He sniffed around, his tail beating against my leg in excitement.

"Festival?" Nick shouted from the kitchen, kneeing the oven door shut, "This place is big, but that's by New York standards."

"It's big enough."

"For fourteen people?"

"Fourteen?"

"Yes, isn't that how many people are coming?"

"Mamí, Papí, tío Julio, tía Sylvia, Danny, Mateo, Sofia, Valerie and her three kids—Adrian, Luis, Carmen…" I lost count, using my thumbs and fingers to keep track. "Some cousins?" I asked Nick, my personal living, breathing, memory bank. I moved the *pascuas* from the windowsill over to the brick wall and bookshelves, shoving an unhung Picasso print to the side.

"Ramon, Paco, and Mateo."

"I already said Mateo."

"Aren't there two of 'em?" Nick questioned, untying his apron, placing it on a hook next to the hanging pans.

I was struggling to put the flowers on the top shelf, standing on my tippy toes as I reached up. "That's right! Yes... one is a priest... never leaves home without his collar, always insists on saying grace. The other is the shortest of the entire family."

"Shorter than you?" Nick asked the back of my neck, licking *dulce* sauce off his thumb. I fell into his chest as he took the flowers, easily placing them on the shelf. I huffed a curl out of my face.

"*Much* shorter than me, but try not to stare... he's so self-conscious of his height... that and his nut allergy... wait—nuts!" I squeaked, flipping around, "Nick, I sprinkled pecans on the tres leches cake!" I pushed him aside, swooping a pile of garland off the coffee table that still needed to be hung. "If a single nut even touches his lips, he'll explode."

"Explode? Sounds dangerous."

"Deadly dangerous."

"Should I warn the neighbors?"

"Nick!" I tossed garland over a steel beam, covering its industrial facade with a more forgiving green touch. "I saw him touch a cashew once... *TOUCH*... and his thumb ballooned into John Goodman."

"Which version? The Flintstones one?"

"I don't know! All the versions combined?" I tried to explain, plugging in the garland. "We can't serve him that cake!" I was totally overwhelmed, piping hot in my black sweater dress, my hair already pinned back in a glittery butterfly clip, keeping it off my shoulders.

Nick turned from the shelf, rolling up the sleeves to his unbuttoned plaid shirt. There wasn't an ounce of sweat or worry on the guy. "Good thing I already baked another *without* pecans." He grinned, totally pleased with himself.

I did a double take, pointing my finger.

"You made another?"

"Just call me St. Nick." He made his way over, his cool hands finding themselves around my bright, red cheeks. "You know I'm always looking after you, baby. You mentioned Mateo's allergy before, just like you mentioned Sofia's fear of dogs... which is why I already moved Marty's treats and toys to the bedroom. He'll be hanging out there tonight. Isn't that right, boy?"

Marty stopped panting, his jingle bell collar silent as he squinted in our direction.

"She's only afraid of chihuahuas, not all dogs. He's fine, you're fine... it's just..." I pulled my head into my hands, wiping down my face, anxious for what was about to come.

I had a secret, and Nick didn't know about it.

My large, loud, very catholic, *very* traditional family from San Juan was traveling over sixteen-hundred miles to see Nick and me in Manhattan.

Exciting?

Yes!

Daunting, and possibly life ruining?

Maybe.

Because there was only one problem with this whole event, a single fact I'd been dreading on telling my family since the moment I knew they were coming.

No one, and I mean no one—not even my own parents—knew that both Nick and I were living together. *What's wrong with that?* Oh, nothing, just that cohabitation was a total sin to my family, not to mention the underlining implication of what living together meant; *if we're sharing a bed, we must be sharing a lot more.*

God, I couldn't even mention the word sex around my mamí, let alone acknowledge the hint of breasts I got at the age of thirteen. Everything felt shameful, but also equally secretive. *Don't ask, don't tell...* well, I was about to tell a whole lot.

"You good, babe?" Nick cradled my chin, giving me a peck on the lips, brushing his nose against mine. I shut my eyes, feeling safe in his hands, but vulnerable with my back to the door, expecting a knock at any moment.

"It's just... this is the first time I'm seeing my family in over two years. Everything has to be perfect and not just for me. I need to show them I still have my roots... my traditions." I rambled, building some defense, assuring myself it was all going to be ok. If I still had traditions, then I could show them that I was still me—the girl who left San Juan, their *good* daughter.

"We got the flowers, the lights... we've been making *pasteles* for the whole week. Do you know how hard it is to find banana leaves in Manhattan?"

"Very..." I added sheepishly, folding my arms into his chest.

"But I found them, didn't I?"

"Mmhmm."

"And aren't they made with love, effort, and *just a tad* of amateur charm?"

"Some *are* skinnier than others."

"Sure, some may look more like cigars than others, but they'll taste just as great."

I laughed as Nick kissed me again, pecking me all over my face and down my neck. His hands moved to my hips, commanding their direction as he swayed me back and forth to an old Marvin Gaye album that played in the background. "You do so much for us... for me." I slowly danced with him, turning my head to rest on his chest.

"What can I say? I love us... I love... you." He kissed my knuckles, his fingers lacing mine. "And I already love your family. They had you, so I know they will be great, because you're phenomenal."

I stayed silent.

I knew they loved me, but could they accept my choices? Wasn't I just allowed to be in love, to be human, to be swept away by something I believed was more real than anything I ever learned in a pew? I respected my family, I respected their beliefs, I just wanted them to respect mine too, and couldn't they?

This wasn't just Nick's apartment anymore, this was my home... *our* home; evident with the photos of us on the wall, us smiling, eating overpriced Bryant Park croissants, wrestling with Marty at Jemmy's Dog Run. This was our life, our beautiful life, and I was in charge of showing it to my family once they arrived. Would living together really cheapen all that? Did sex—the one thing we didn't talk about growing up—mean that much to them? Couldn't they see my happiness, my books mixed with Nick's, my candles burning in his foyer, my plants hanging from his cabinets? We were intertwined, we were dancing, literally, on top of my rug, that sat below his couch.

"Being traditional is just really important to them. I'm sensitive to how they'll react to certain things..."

"Like what?" Nick nodded to a counter full of sesame chicken and pork fried rice. "I know Chinese food isn't part of a typical Puerto Rican Christmas, but I'm thinking it's kind of ours now, right?"

"How could it not be? You know I count that night in the elevator as our first date."

"Good, because I do, too. Speaking of which, are egg rolls an aphrodisiac?"

"Oh, stop!" I bit my lip, giving his ass a squeeze.

He chuckled in my ear.

"Seriously. What is it about Sichuan Garden? It's like every time we eat there we fool around."

"I think it's the memories more than the food." I kissed his arms, squeezing him tight as he lifted me in the air. He spun me around, setting me back on my feet. "But I agree... there's something about their noodles."

"Is it the slurping?"

"*Sucking*," I emphasized, entranced by Nick's fingertip tracing up my thigh, lifting my dress.

"Lots of sucking, huh, naughty-list girl?" His hand cupped my ass, taking advantage of how my thong barely covered my flesh. I was hot again, but enjoyably so, savoring how Nick kissed me slowly. "This is our tradition, and it's not all about the sex. It's about being honest with you, about how you've always meant more to me than anyone else. It's about how I finally told you how I felt." He nodded to a pyramid of fortune cookies. "It's not just about the past, it's about where we're going..."

To hell? I thought.

Nick was right. Our newly formed tradition of Chinese food for Christmas was landmarked by memories of a year full of hot, premarital, sinful—oh, so delicious—sex. I couldn't unsee it; sucking his cock on the couch, the time he fucked my ass on the kitchen counter, the window he pressed my tits against while eating me out. This house was a shrine of love, and a reminder of what would most likely give my abuelita a heart attack. OH, god, the bedroom! While giving them a tour, they'd surely see our bed, the spot where Nick and I fucked at least three times a week. How could I show them that? How could I point and say, '*This is our bed, this is where we turn into animals and make noises that scare Marty'?*

Ugh!

None of this would be weird if we'd only been more open as a family, if the topic of sex wasn't treated like some fragile bomb of conversation. Did I even hide my dildos? I needed to put them away, because my cousins were total snoops, and I wouldn't put it past them to check my nightstand.

Shit, it all made me so nauseous.

"Nick, there's something I—"

Nick's hand pulled up to the small of my back, his hard body pressed against mine. "I know you're stressed, baby. I promise everything will be ok. Look at us, what's not to love? Even the priest will be smitten."

"Priest? Mateo!"

"Mateo number 1," Nick assured.

"No! Oh, shit, the Nativity! Nick!" I pulled away, scurrying. "They're going to be here any minute and I forgot to set it up!"

"We got coquito! That should help."

I rushed to the unopened Nativity box, impatiently biting into the plastic wrap. "It's not enough. I'm not even sure *this* is enough."

"Why not? Why are you so panicked?"

Marty barked.

"Because... there are expectations."

"Is it our home? Our linens? What expectations? Wait, are you secretly royalty?" he asked suspiciously, being playful as I spat out a chunk of plastic.

"No, Nick, not royalty, just... *royally* dead! They're expecting to come to my home, to my living room, to my bed where I live and sleep alone. My parents don't know we live together!"

"What?" he scrunched his brow.

Marty wagged his tail.

"Yes, I know! It's just... there's never been a good time to tell them. I got promoted, we fell in love, we moved in."

"Yes. Good, good, good. Those sound like positives to me."

"And they are, but they don't believe in this..." I motioned around the entire apartment. Nick followed my hands, confused as I pointed to the walls.

"Believe in what? Bricks?" he laughed.

"No. In us, living together... *sleeping together*." I whispered, still struggling with the Nativity.

"You mean sex?"

"Uh, no, Nick, not just sex! Fucking. We've fucked *everywhere*. This place is a love nest, it's evidence to what I am: a living, breathing, sexually active woman!"

Nick pursed his lips, furrowing. "We have fourteen people coming to our apartment, most of whom are your cousins to the same couple... I think they know *all* about fucking."

"Yes, Catholics fuck, but we don't talk about it... or at least my family doesn't."

"So the Nativity will fix this?" he asked, confused. "You don't even believe in it, and you still want it up?"

"I'm just trying," I said pathetically, as Nick came to help.

"Here, let me open that up."

"I got it, trust me."

"You don't. If I can just—"

I gasped as I yanked on the Nativity, dropping it, falling back into the pyramid of fortune cookies. The large styrofoam lid popped open, as a scattering of sheep and wise men rolled along the constellation of unwrapped cookies.

"Oh, shit!" I covered my mouth. "The baby! Where's the baby Jesus?"

"There, there!" Nick pointed as we both dropped to our knees.

"Why is he blonde with blue eyes?" I asked

mildly panicked, my hand splayed across the floor as I crawled to him.

"I don't know? Immaculate adoption?" Nick cringed, trying to get to me as fast as he could, "Wait, Elena just don't—"

Nick stopped his sentence as I froze.

Stunned.

Speechless.

The room got incredibly quiet, the record in the background ended, and Marty scurried away. My heart pounded in my chest.

"Oh my god, Nick." My eyes welled with hot tears, my curls falling loose from my butterfly clip. Right at my knees, beside Jesus, smashed open from a fortune cookie, was a ring. But not just any ring...

A small.

Perfect.

Diamond ring.

Nick squeezed his face shut, taking a deep breath. "It was going to be a surprise." He closed his eyes, before peeking up apologetically.

"Is this?"

"It is. Elena... I love you. I've loved you since the moment I met you. I knew it then, I know it now, here, in this home we built, in the life we live. And I know it's quick, and I know it may not be traditional... but I want it for the rest of my life. My forever begins with you, and it ends with you... and nothing could ever make me believe otherwise. What we have... it was always meant to be." He picked up the ring, propping himself on one knee as I sat before him, crying.

"Do you mean that?" I looked into his eyes, surrounded by what others would assume was just a scattering of old, stale, novelty cookies—they were anything but. They were pieces of us, of our story, and for as many traditions as I once had, new ones were forming, and that meant everything to me. Nick wasn't just my former neighbor, my current boyfriend, or the man of my dreams... he was my home, and if being loved for who I was and what I did was the pillar of what family meant, then I certainly had that with Nick.

"I do mean it... I was just waiting for your family to get here... to get your father's permission. I wanted to surprise you in front of everyone, I wanted—"

"Yes." My lip quivered, answering him already. It wasn't about a ring; it wasn't about marriage. It was about love; it was about being accepted with no conditions. That was Nick. "I will..."

Nick didn't even have to ask, slipping the ring on my finger, pulling me in for the longest kiss we'd ever shared. I laughed, I cried, but most of all I felt relieved as a knock came from the front door.

"You ready, naughty-list girl?" Nick smiled, thumbing away a tear. I looked at the door, knowing that regardless of the ring I was just given, that I was going to be proud of my truth—a truth I would admit to with no shame or regard for reactions. This was *our* life, *our* home, and I knew whatever was to come by opening that door, that Nick Stafford—the man of my dreams—would always be by my side.

I loved him.

I always would.

And now, we would face everything together.

"I'm ready." I kissed him. "I'll always be ready."

The End.

Still in the holiday mood? Read Gemma and Parker's bonus chapter from the Mine to Keep series as they venture through a booze-filled, endearing, and fun New Year's Eve, *after author's note.*

Did you enjoy Merry Little Mishap? Did you know reviews/ratings help indie authors be noticed by more readers?

If you enjoyed this book, please spread the love on your favorite platform with a review! It can be short and sweet, or anything you wish. Thank you for reading.

Author's Note

Elena Ortiz had a huge job to do for *New York Prestige*, and that was to rank the hottest sex toys for the holiday season. But all of that didn't come without its complications.

Shame, culture, and religion all played a pivotal role in the creation of this quirky novella, and though it's lighthearted, there were some real-life feelings (and personal experiences) that I wanted to share with you.

* * *

I'll never forget it. I was eight years old when I first saw Leonardo DiCaprio sketch a very voluptuous, very nude Kate Winslet in the middle of Titanic. There I was, blocked from some forbidden sight, my mother's right hand in a bag of popcorn, her left one over my eyes.

"Don't peek," she whispered.

But I peeked anyways. And why wouldn't I?

What was so horrible—or so incredible—that I had to be shielded from her—a woman that hundreds of other people stared at, who was sprawled over a massive screen in a dark movie theatre?

We were front and center after all, and things got even more interesting when poor man Jack took Rose in the back of that old Coupé de Ville. There was no disguising the sound of her hand slapping onto that steamy window, nor the strange panting that proceeded. And before you wonder any further, the answer is yes... I peeked at that, too. Didn't you?

Sex. That's what I was guarded from, my eyes constantly instructed to be shut anytime the slightest hint of intimacy would appear on TV or a movie.

I think my family was trying to keep me away from it, but without context their attempts only magnified my curiosity! Why couldn't I look? Why did I want to? And why did it feel kinda good (yet bad) to do so?

These weren't easy questions to answer, especially since sex wasn't something my family ever talked about, let alone acknowledged. Why was that?

Sex is seemingly everywhere, slapped on every product, movie, show, advertisement, even cartoons (let's not pretend we all didn't feel something, when

Jasmine came out in that little red two piece in Aladdin), yet, I knew nothing about it growing up, except of course two things:

1. **Sex is naughty** (and not in the way we like in our books).

2. **Sex isn't to be talked about...** (so don't even bring it up... in fact, disregard point number one! Since we can't talk about it, then we can't possibly think about it, therefore, why ask questions?)

Growing up in a religious, traditionally Hispanic family with lots of siblings, cousins, tíos (uncles), and tías (aunts), was a strange setting for the lack of sex talk, especially since everyone seemed to be having it!

(And don't get me started on the paradox of sex being taboo in my family, while the topic of when I was going to have children was openly discussed).

So what did I do with these questions, feelings, and curiosities at a young age? I explored them, of course, but I did so in secrecy—and secrecy led to embarrassment and shame.

That was a lot to carry as an adolescent, not to mention as an adult, who didn't realize that this was just unresolved guilt from a subject that others felt uncomfortable discussing.

Writing Elena Ortiz and introducing family issues surrounding sexual shame, generational guilt, and the complex feelings that surrounded them, felt like an important part of my upbringing that I wanted to explore.

Elena tackled this issue from a Latinx perspective, which includes unresolved cultural pressures that stem from religious and societal beliefs on sex. But the truth is, this complex issue reaches far past my own experiences as a Latina, and spans to every culture, race, and religion around the world.

Having a character explore her sexuality while balancing an idea of staying true to familial values can be a daunting subject to tackle, but it felt important for me to do so, because reclaiming the meaning of sexuality is a healing tool that helps counter—what I believe to be—a hijacked understanding of what it means to be human.

Sex is multifaceted and natural; it's self-exploration, self-love and self-care. It can be healing and beautiful, romantic and sensual, but it can also be primal and cathartic, which is just as valid.

The truth is, it can be all the things listed above, because that's the beauty of being human, and we get a lifetime to explore and challenge the beliefs that we have always been told were wrong—such as: sex is evil, masturbation is dirty, or that female pleasure is only a lucky byproduct of something more biological, i.e. sex is only for having babies.

I hope you found some solace in Elena's struggles, and some peace in her epilogue, because if you grew up anything like me, then you could understand the difficulty of what even an innocent sex toy being delivered to your door can cause in your life (let alone stealing a peek of Kate Winslet's beautiful body).

Love always,
Vivian Mae

NEW YEARS EVE - 2015
GEMMA

"Someday all your dreams will come true, Gemma! Worlds will crash! Stars will align! Everyone will know your name... but only *one* man will take it and turn it into his!" Dana looped her arm in mine as we stumbled up the icy block near 94th Street and Madison Avenue. Our fur coats squeezed together like tussled bears caught in a kiss.

"Marriage?!" I asked far too loudly, my heels skidding on ice as Dana held on tighter, her blonde pinned back waves bouncing.

"Ring. On. The. Finger." She snapped with each word, the noise muted by her leather gloves. "Don't get me wrong... it'll be complicated I'm sure, but men will one hundred percent fight over you."

"Yeah, right!"

"I'm serious. They will! You're a complex girl, Gem, with a complex future. And trust me, I *knooooow* these things." She slurred her last line, her large, brown eyes catching every glowing dot of Christmas lights hung along the brownstones, and woody Irish pubs.

Dana Myers was not only my roommate at FIT, but she was also a self-proclaimed cupid in the making. As if being born on Valentine's Day wasn't enough, Dana's ego was bolstered by the successful pairing of fifteen different couples in her short lifetime; three from when she was in middle school, eight from high school, and the other four from our time at the Fashion Institute of Technology.

"You'll be married long before you hit your thirties."

"That's not far off!" I squeaked, holding in a burp that tasted like orange juice and grenadine.

Dana's head bobbed into mine, drunk. "You'll see. It'll be perfect. The man will be tall. Handsome. He'll have money and charm. He'll push you out of your comfort zone, but also, challenge everything you ever believed about love." Dana squeezed my arm tighter, "This man will accept you for who you are, and for who you'll become... because when you look at him, not only will you see yourself, but you'll see your future—which will be the best version of you possible." Dana carried the cadence of an angel, mixed with a carnival barker.

She was selling me on an idea, a promise of what could be possible. Could all that really be true for me? I wanted to believe her, and whether or not Dana could really predict the future, I appreciated her effort. It was a much kinder and more insightful version than what Claire, my mother, ever gave me. I tried not to think of her—alone in Bushwick, stewing by the phone, waiting to call me before the New Year's countdown to warn me about the terrors of kissing a guy who'd eventually break my heart.

I *knew* I wouldn't be able to handle that call tonight, let alone her repeated stories of my father and their mess of a marriage. Her dark, dark history sat buried in my stomach, piled on by shots of tequila I forcibly drank because of her inevitable phone call.

However, Claire wasn't the only reason I'd been drinking tonight.

There was something else.

I had a huge decision to make by tomorrow morning, one that'd change my life in a significant way.

"Do you think David could be the one?" I asked Dana, who smiled happily for no reason, until I brought up his name.

"Ew! No," she recoiled with a sour face.

Dana had never been a fan of David. They met just a few months ago, but all it took for her to dislike him was a sweaty handshake. Dana claimed to be spiritually connected, feeling some *off* vibes about him, but he'd been nothing short of a gentleman around me.

"No?" I asked. "What do you mean? And don't bring up his aftershave again. It smells nice... when it's not so strong."

"I don't know, Gem, he doesn't give off soulmate vibes. You two aren't really a match."

"You're gonna have to start liking him, he'll be around us more."

"Oh, god, please don't tell me—"

"If we got married, you and I would have the same last name," I laughed, cutting her off to avoid an incoming insult, "We could be sisters!"

"We're not even related! There's lots of people with the last name Myers, and he so happens to be giving the rest of us a bad rep."

"Look," I lifted my thumb up, counting out a list of pros, "He's already graduated, he's got money. He's got charm—"

"He *texts* in all caps," Dana cut me off. "Every conversation we have comes back to bitcoin, and that's not even the worst part..." I rolled my eyes, I had a feeling I knew what she was about to say, but kept my mouth shut, because I couldn't exactly defend David on this one. "This man-child ordered a glass of milk with his filet last week at Del Frisco's."

Yup... let's gloss over that fact.

"He's an accountant! David's good with money, and compared to many of his colleagues, he's still got a great set of hair. Plus, he's the one that snuck us into the bar tonight... well, snuck you into the bar," I argued, scrunching at the snow flurries that tapped my nose.

Dana hated being the only one under the drinking age, but she wasn't far behind. She didn't mind the favor, but she knew David was just trying to butter her up.

"If I have to like the guy, then whatever, but I need to ask you a super important question..."

"Here we go."

"I'm serious, Gem! Humor me for a sec."

"Fine," I waved, still following one foot in front of the other on the semi-icy pavement.

"Does he make you come?" Dana asked.

"What?!" I stammered, shrugging, "We're doing *ok* in that department. Don't worry about that."

It wasn't a detailed conversation I wanted to have while walking in front of the boys—none of whom were David. I tried to keep my voice down, not wanting them to hear... this was especially true for the man directly behind me, whose name I didn't even want to think about because it made me smile like an idiot. If Dana even noticed the difference in my expression, she'd call me out on it.

"What do you mean, '*ok in that department*'?" Dana's *ew* voice came back. "It's sex, Gemma, not a sector in the corporate ladder. The man you're meant to be with will rock your socks... and your box," she said crudely, laughing.

"We're doing okay in bed, the sex is truly just fine. You know orgasms aren't my speciality, unless I'm by myself. Besides, these things take time, and time is what we'll have soon... once-we-move-in-together-next-month," I spat out as fast as possible.

Dana hated the idea, and she knew David wasn't the one, her eyes darting over her shoulder to the tallest, most athletic, track star in all of Columbia University—as if he were the only right choice for me. Not only was he the complete opposite of David, but he was my childhood best friend since first grade—an all star law student and legal savant whose eyes had been pinned to the back of my head since the moment we left the bar that David snuck us into.

It was *Parker Ellis Jones*.

The boy I grew up with.

The boy I dreamed of having... since... well...

since dreams of mine ever existed—and my god did I fucking actually *dream* of him.

I glanced over my shoulder, still stumbling, catching his unbroken attention—his emerald glossy eyes rapturing my heart into a—*oh my god I've been caught*—racing pulse. Damnit, I was thinking of him again and I had that stupid, idiotic smile on my face. Dana saw it and grinned.

"You're not supposed to be Gemma. Rose. Harrison-Myers... you're supposed to be Gemma. Rose. Harrison-*Jones*—world's most famous fashion designer."

"Oh-my-god-Dana!" I screeched quickly, mortified by how she unabashedly attached Parker's last name to mine.

"You're only with David because he has hair like Parker... and that's only on his *good hair days*, mind you," she argued. "You and Parker are end game. You two are Monica and Chandler, Jim and Pam, Robin and Barney."

"Try Bert and Ernie," I stopped her. "Strictly platonic..." I batted my eyes, unwilling to accept any other truth at the moment.

Parker was my entire world, had been since the field trip to the Majestic Theatre where we first met, and there was so much history compacted into our tiny existence, that even the thought of telling him how I felt became the most untouchable topic in my head.

Don't go there.

Don't chance it.

I could live with not telling Parker about how I felt, but I couldn't live with potentially losing him over my—most likely unreciprocated—feelings.

"Bert and Ernie are totally not platonic... even I knew that as a child. Besides, Parker is totally into you."

"Into me being his best friend. That's all we've been," I stood my ground, trudging past tossed out Christmas trees and crinkled flyers for the Times Square ball drop party tonight.

"He's the one. Not David," Dana said.

"No. Also. I couldn't even *try* and chance that."

"Why not?"

"It's too risky," I shook my head.

"Riskier than moving in with *Mr. Milk For Dinner?*"

"I just have a very complicated stance on love." I wasn't willing to go into the depths of my reasons, or how they were tied to my mother, who essentially terrified me from ever getting *too* close to others. No one knew about her mantra's; her warnings, the late nights and terrible days in a manic depressive spiral about how my father leaving us ruined our lives—my life.

I couldn't explain to Dana what that felt like, how even the thought of my mother made my throat swell with anxiety.

"We need a vote," Dana declared. "How does everyone feel about David?" she turned to ask Parker, spinning me free.

My legs gave out, my heels slipping on ice as I fell backwards, screaming into the air before slamming onto the freezing pavement.

But that didn't happen.

My legs left the floor, and my body floated into the heat of two strong arms.

"Gotcha, Butterfly." Parker didn't break his pace, his unbendable, deep voice soothed me with a dimpled smirk that I instantly wanted to kiss. *Craved* to kiss.

"Spinning out like fucking Tanya Harding." Tommy—Parker's closest frat brother, and universally loved smart ass—blew into his hands, keeping them warm. His eyes were about as glossy and red as hard cherry candies. "You almost killed her, Dana. And you call me a klutz."

"I never called you a klutz, you jerk! I've called you a lot of things—"

"Please, don't list them—" Tommy shot back.

"Inconsiderate!" Dana swatted Tommy with her leopard clutch for each word she started to list, "home wrecker, player, scum..."

"You forgot charming, funny, and hung like a horse." Tommy smiled to himself, a young but debonaire expression that made Dana's cheeks radiant pink.

It wasn't surprising they were like this.

Dana—the essential star gazing, fortune-telling, matchmaker was incapable of tolerating the chaotic, sexcapade fueled reputation of Tommy Romero. Having them meet at one of Dana's matchmaking parties was a terrible idea, especially since Tommy solely went with the intention of grabbing as much free food and phone numbers as possible; not for love.

"Promise to never hit me as hard as Dana hits Tommy. No matter how badly I mess up," Parker curled me up to his lips, whispering behind my ear. "*I think they like it, though... so maybe it's not so bad,*" he added, his words hitting my neck like a summer day in December.

"Just don't drop me. And we'll be good," I answered.

"Like this?" Parker pretended to buckle, my auburn waves falling loose from my beret, and over his arms. I screamed so loud the entire block heard.

"Parker Jones, don't you dare!" I exclaimed.

He paused.

And smiled.

"Dare what? Let you go? I'd never do that." Heat blossomed below my breast as Parker's fingers secured me further, firmly cupping the spot above my ribs, and upper thigh.

I stared speechless and drunk, admiring how his dimpled cheeks were the only soft feature on his strong face; a chin peppered with a five o'clock shadow, and a furrow that lightened up from the exorbitant amount of booze we had.

God, I could die in his arms and be happy.

Did I really just think that?

Wait, did I say that out loud?

No. But I kind of wanted to! I loved him, and I also loved his family, a family I spent a lifetime growing up with—people who gave me the only sense of security I strived for. He was everything I wanted, but also, everything I couldn't risk losing.

"I'm thinking drinking as many *Tequila Sunrises* before the sun *actually* rises was a mistake," I smiled into his chest. "Are you ok carrying me?"

"Of course. I can carry *all* four Gemma's I'm seeing right now." Parker swiped his tongue over his lip, his eyes trying not to shut, way past the point of being buzzed. He and David had far more drinks than the rest of us, and after a while their friendly first meeting began to feel competitive. They pounded drinks back and forth until David began sweating through his work shirt, sopping his silk tie with the smell of booze.

At least Parker didn't leave the bar smelling like one, his scent heady and warm, perfectly crisp like the center of a new leather billfold, but reminiscent of the mahogany wood that lined his fraternity's chapter house.

"What are we voting on now?" Tommy rolled his eyes, finishing some argument he and Dana had along the snowy path.

"We're asking how everyone felt about David tonight! I've met him before... but you two haven't." Dana pointed her clutch at both Parker and Tommy, directing them like a general of love and war.

"I like anyone who'll pay for my drinks," Tommy answered immediately. "Plus he gave me great financial advice. Has anyone heard of bitcoin?"

"Oh my god, stop. Stop. Stop." Dana squished Tommy's mouth shut. "Parker?" she asked, seeking some form of approval.

I wanted their meeting to go right, even if David and I had only been together a few months. I was always hesitant for the day he'd meet Parker; the man I compared him to, not that I'd ever tell Dana that. I guess them meeting was what made the idea of moving in with David feel real, and real was terrifying, because I cared so much about what Parker thought. I wasn't sure how he felt about David yet, but he looked happy, that was, before his face faltered.

Parker cleared his throat.

"To be fair, he seemed nice," he said briskly, like the admission wasn't his favorite.

"Nice?" Dana asked as we reached Parker and Tommy's frat house, stepping up a stoop and entering inside. "Nice is Gemma, the girl who insisted on walking you both home instead of going back to David's apartment right away."

Parker carried me through the doorway, his fingers tucking my head gently into his chest so I wouldn't hit the wood frame. It was like we were married, and believe me, the fantasy didn't escape me as I pictured it perfectly—as if it were our wedding night.

"She wanted to take us home? She's the one that fell!" Tommy made his way over to the makeshift bar cart, fishing out red solo cups and a bottle of cheap rum and soda.

"I. Am. Drunk," I said slowly, pointing my finger in the air as Parker stood me back up.

He flopped right onto the couch, kicking off his

boots. He lied down with his coat still on, his burgundy scarf loosened around his broad shoulders.

"We're all drunk!" Tommy shooed away, pouring us fresh drinks.

Parker pushed his cup away. "God, no. I've had too much tequila at the bar. I'll never let you talk me into drinking that again, Gemma. That's the worst shit ever," he teased and smiled.

Dana made her way to the fireplace, tossing in a few logs of wood, lighting them with a match. The whole room was set aglow, the ancient fraternity illuminated in all its glory; old leather furniture, hand carved banisters, and built-in bookshelves stacked with law texts that the fraternity shared.

I made my way around the coffee table to a tufted green chair, but Parker caught me by the wrist and pulled me towards him.

My face grew so hot as I squealed, my back landing right in the middle of his hard body, the nook of his thighs and pelvis the perfect spot to sit between.

"Come here! I'm cold, and I'm stealing your warmth," Parker wrapped his hands around my stomach, softly squeezing me like a pillow.

This was normal.

We did this all the time in the Hamptons while vacationing with his family.

The sleepovers.

The movie nights.

DON'T look into this hug, Gemma, I told myself.

"Ok... so David is nice. Granted I think he's all wrong for Gemma," Dana began. "Did everyone know he's asking her to move in with him?"

"Whoa!" Tommy raised his red cup, "That's awesome, Gem! Guess that means we're going to have a new drinking buddy around."

Parker tensed against me, his fingers like possessive claws that secured me harder. His voice dropped. "Move in?" he asked.

"Yeah. Over to Brooklyn. As in past the bridge. He wants her to take the subway to school," Dana noted.

"Lots of people take the subway. It's New York," I tried to play it down. Parker hated the idea of me riding the subway, because—as he's told me multiple times—people got mugged, pushed onto the tracks, or jerked off in front of while riding to their stop. "He's over in Brooklyn now. I'm taking the subway tonight over there—"

"Absolutely not," Parker jumped in, "There's no way in hell you're taking the subway alone. On New Year's Eve?"

"David is expecting me. We have plans."

"David bailed at the bar to go to a work gathering…"

"It was for business!" I defended.

Parker shook his head against me, "It was an office party. The guy should've invited you. No. He should've *insisted* on having you there—showing you off—bragging to others about how fucking great his New Year's is going to be, simply because you're by his side."

"I know I would," Tommy took a long sip. "Who is she supposed to kiss on New Year's now…" Tommy didn't even hide the fact that he winked right at Parker.

Did Tommy know something I didn't, or was this just another one of his dumb jokes? I mean, Parker had never made a move in all our years of being friends, so why would he now?

Dana smacked him again with her clutch. "Gemma can't move in with David! And he's expecting an answer by tomorrow. His lease is up."

"That's fast," Tommy nodded.

"Too fast," Parker added, a tad anxious sounding.

My phone buzzed in my coat, and my heart dropped. I figured it was my mother, sending her godawful New Year's message of doom.

But it wasn't, it was David.

His message popped up on my screen, *all in caps.*

. . .

DAVID MYERS

U COMING? I'M SO FCKN
HRNY!!

I pulled the phone into my chest, covering it with my fuzzy coat. Oh my god, I hope Parker didn't see that.

Really, David?

And in all caps, too?

"I'd like to change my stance on David," Parker announced sharply. "Him expecting you to come out in the middle of the night, alone on a train to his place in Brooklyn is insane."

"I'm an adult," I defended. "I can manage just fine."

"This isn't about being an adult. You're Gemma. *My* Gemma. The girl who was afraid of cats in the fifth grade after watching Pet Semetery. And it doesn't matter whether you think you'll be safe or not, I've always been there to keep monsters away from you." He went to stand, but wobbled, clutching onto the back of the sofa to balance himself.

"You're drunk!" I said.

"We're all drunk," Tommy repeated.

"Yes. Yes. Drunk, but not stupid... stupid as in asking Gemma to come over right now, across the entire city and the bridge. Would he even be waiting for you at the stop?" Parker looked at me for an answer.

I wasn't sure.

I blinked. "He's only a few blocks away from the station."

Parker ran his hand down his chiseled face, his dirty blonde hair sprung into cute ducktails as he swopped it back in disbelief. "A few blocks away? Dressed as you are? No."

"Dressed like what?" I asked, sitting up, holding Parker as he tried to get his balance.

"Like... like... you..." was all Parker could say.

"Like a hottie!" Tommy added, then scrunched his nose.

"Not that it matters. Most men are pigs and monsters, and it's hardly safe to be out during the day, let alone late at night," Parker said annoyed.

"Yup!" Tommy interrupted. "I'd like to change my mind on David, too. I heard he drinks milk with his steak."

"First smart thing you've said tonight," Dana agreed.

"You heard that?" I squeaked, mortified that Parker and Tommy overheard my conversation with Dana.

Parker massaged his temples, "We heard it all…" he took a few steps forward, "I'm calling us a cab, Mrs. Harrison-Jones. I'm taking you myself."

Parker barely made it to the spiraling wood banister before I scolded him, "Would you wait! You're too drunk to go upstairs."

"My phone is up there. I'm fine."

"If I can't go to Brooklyn alone, then you can't go upstairs alone. Don't argue with me about that." I wasn't any better, stammering in his direction as we both leaned on each other like dying mountain climbers.

It was just us in the house, all the other brothers were out for the holidays, leaving the upstairs particularly dark and quiet.

"Why'd you drink so much more than the rest of us, anyways?" I asked, helping Parker to his bed.

"Because of David." He collapsed onto his comforter, before searching the nightstand for his phone. "I couldn't let him beat me at drinking."

"That's so dumb," I laughed.

"Dumb people do dumb things."

"Yeah, but you're not *dumb people*. Scholarship-winning law students don't need to win drinking contests with entry level tax accountants."

"So you're admitting I won," he smiled fondly, and swiped at his phone. "I guess I get the prize…"

I sat next to him, getting cold upstairs away from the fire. His bed was filled with blankets, and the heater kicked on above us, blowing the first remnants of cold air that picked at my cheeks.

"What prize were you expecting?" I asked curiously, hypnotized by green haunting eyes, his breath sweet with tequila and spearmint.

Fireworks went off in the distance.

Popping.

Exploding into radiant sulfuric reds and greens just outside Parker's window. The colors and sparkles caught the contours of his cheeks and gaze.

"I get to be the first to tell you Happy New Year," he whispered, his greeting needy and hot.

His hand fell on mine, raising it up to his lips, then he combed back the sleeve of my fuzzy jacket. Hot fingertips teased the length of my arm, leaving trails of goosebumps that followed as he delicately kissed my hand.

A kiss I wondered about.

A kiss that felt innocent yet indulgent, tender, desperate.

"Happy New Year," I whispered back, drawing near his face, my lip trembling.

I wanted to kiss him, and oh my god, I think he wanted to kiss me, too! It would be our first kiss. Real kiss. All to the orchestrated tone of Auld Lang Syne downstairs and outside. And as we grew closer my phone buzzed again in my pocket.

I felt it.

So did Parker, and he looked down at it.

"If you're wondering if it's your mom... it's not," he said quietly.

I shook my head. "I, uh... I was hoping she wouldn't call... but every year it's the same—"

"I know," he smiled, his large hand swallowing mine, squeezing it. "I used Tommy's phone to call her at the bar. Told her Happy New Year... and that you forgot your phone. I know you dread it, and I just wanted to help."

I was surprised by the tears in my eyes. If anyone listened to me, if anyone knew how to protect me from the world, it was Parker. It always was. I was sure David was texting me, but I didn't want to see it —I didn't want to see anything other than what the future held in Parker's eyes.

"You did that for me?" I pouted.

"You're a promise that I'll never break. I'll keep you safe, Butterfly, no matter what it costs me..." His forehead met mine, "Please, don't let me go. Don't go to David's. There's so many of him out there... but there's only one of you. And I know that's not fair for me to ask that of you, but keeping you safe isn't just what I told your mother on the phone I'd do... it's what my heart begs me for every day." He shut his eyes, slowly leaning back, his hands cradling my shoulders, pulling me into his body. He lied back in bed, and took me with him, and I never felt more safe. "I drank too much... and I've said too little." I heard him smile.

"You've said enough." My heart bloomed for this man. He held me so tight, I could fall asleep right here, knowing that in the end, we'd always be together. "You're my best friend, Parker Jones."

"You're mine, too... Gemma Jones..." he said, giving me his last name again, his eyes shut, passing out into a tequila sunrise coma that warmed his body against mine.

Gemma Rose Jones.

I loved that.

I wanted that.

Which was why I needed to break up with David first thing in the morning.

This would be my year, and before graduation I'd finally tell Parker how I really felt.

I was in love. And nothing could stop me from getting my happily ever after.

...

·   ·   ·

Continue reading Gemma and Parker's story in this spicy, friends to lovers, age gap love triangle that'll leave you shocked with its twists and turns. Read today.

MORE BY VIVIAN MAE

<u>*Mine to Keep Series*</u>

Lawsuit and Leather (book 1)

Promise and Punishment (book 2)

Arrogant, brooding, and impossibly insistent action star, Alex Rivers, is determined to pull Gemma Harrison out of her insecure shell, but there's only one problem, her childhood best friend, and New York's fiercest lawyer, Parker Jones, is in the way.

Burning Little Secrets

A secret romance filled with devious secrets, angsty lure and breath hitching steam. Burning Little Secrets divulges the forbidden journey of an engaged woman's encounter with a sexy small town hero.

FREAK

A short enemies to lovers romance filled with oh-so-sweet revenge, and hot smut. FREAK dives into the journey of a scorned woman's encounter with her high school bully ten years later.

About the Author

Vivian Mae is a Latina indie author, living out of Phoenix, AZ who writes sexy contemporary romance for her naughty readers.

She is married to her best friend, fulfilling her own trope of best friends to lovers.

When she isn't writing, you can find her laughing alongside her husband, binging trashy TV, sneaking chocolates, reading her favorite naughty novels, and dreaming about pizza and wine.

Subscribe to my newsletter for exclusive updates:

https://www.vivianmae.com/newsletter

Facebook Reader Group - Vivian Mae's Babes

Follow me on social media, let's connect and chat books and your favorite characters!

9 781962 659031